W9-BON-283

Harlequin Presents®

UNCUT

Even more passion for your reading pleasure!

Escape into a world of intense passion and
scorching romance! You'll find the drama,
the emotion, the international settings and
happy endings that you've always loved in
Harlequin Presents® novels. But we've turned
up the thermostat just a little, so that the
relationships really sizzle. Careful, they're
almost too hot to handle!

Look for some of your favorite bestselling
authors in the UNCUT miniseries!

Sarah Morgan

Million-Dollar Love-Child

UNcut

HARLEQUIN®

TORONTO • NEW YORK • LONDON
AMSTERDAM • PARIS • SYDNEY • HAMBURG
STOCKHOLM • ATHENS • TOKYO • MILAN • MADRID
PRAGUE • WARSAW • BUDAPEST • AUCKLAND

ISBN-13: 978-0-373-12582-1
ISBN-10:   0-373-12582-8

MILLION-DOLLAR LOVE-CHILD

First North American Publication 2006.

All about the author...
Sarah Morgan

SARAH MORGAN was born in Wiltshire and started writing at the age of eight when she produced an autobiography of her hamster.

At the age of eighteen she traveled to London to train as a nurse in one of London's top teaching hospitals, and she describes what happened in those years as extremely happy and definitely censored! She worked in a number of areas in the hospital after she qualified.

Over time her writing interests had moved on from hamsters to men, and she started creating romance fiction. Her first completed manuscript, written after the birth of her first child, was rejected by Harlequin, but the comments were encouraging, so she tried again; on the third attempt her manuscript *Worth the Risk* was accepted unchanged. She describes receiving the acceptance letter as one of the best moments of her life, after meeting her husband and having her two children.

Sarah still works part-time in a health-related industry and spends the rest of the time with her family trying to squeeze in writing whenever she can. She is an enthusiastic skier and walker, and loves outdoor life.

To Kim Young, for being a great friend
and a fantastic editor.
Thank you.

CHAPTER ONE

SHE'D never known fear like it.

Breathing so rapidly that she felt light-headed, Kimberley stood in the imposing glass-walled boardroom on the executive floor of Santoro Investments, staring down at the throbbing, vibrant streets of Rio de Janeiro.

The waiting was torture.

Everything rested on the outcome of this visit—*everything*—and the knowledge made her legs weaken and her insides knot with vicious tension.

It was ironic, she thought helplessly, that the only person who could help her now was the one man she'd sworn never to see again.

Forcing herself to breathe steadily, she closed her eyes for a moment and tried to modify her expectations. He'd probably refuse to see her.

People didn't just arrive unannounced and gain access to a man like Luc Santoro.

She was only sitting here now because his personal assistant had taken pity on her. Stammering out her request to see him, Kimberley had been so pale and anxious that the older woman had become quite concerned and had insisted that she should sit and wait in the privacy of the air-conditioned boardroom. Having brought her a large glass of water, the assistant

had given her a smile and assured her that Mr Santoro really
wasn't as dangerous as his reputation suggested.

But Kimberley knew differently. Luc Santoro wasn't just
dangerous, he was lethal and she knew that it was going to
take more than water to make her face the man on the other
side of that door.

What was she going to say?

How was she going to tell him?

Where was she going to start?

She couldn't appeal to his sense of decency or his conscience because he possessed neither. Helping others wasn't
high on his agenda. He *used* people and, more especially, he
used women. She knew that better than anyone. Pain ripped
through her as she remembered just how badly he'd treated
her. He was a ruthless, self-seeking billionaire with only one
focus in his life. The pursuit of pleasure.

And for a short, blissful time, she'd been his pleasure.

Her heart felt like a heavy weight in her chest. Looking
back on it now, she couldn't believe how naïve she'd been.
How trusting. As an idealistic, romantic eighteen-year-old,
she'd been willing and eager to share every single part of herself with him. She'd held nothing back because she'd seen no
reason to hold anything back. He'd been the one. Her everything. *And she'd been his nothing.*

She curled her fingers into her palms and reminded herself that the objective of today was not to rehash the past. She
was going to have to put aside the memory of the pain, the
panic and the bone-deep humiliation she'd suffered as a result of his cruel and careless rejection.

None of that mattered now.

There was only one thing that mattered to her, *only one
person*, and for the sake of that person she was going to bite
her tongue, smile, beg or do whatever it took to ingratiate her-

self with Luc Santoro—because there was no way she was leaving Brazil without the money she needed.

It was a matter of life and death.

She paced the length of the room, trying to formulate some sort of plan in her mind, trying to work out a reasonable way to ask for five million dollars from a man who had absolutely no feelings for her.

How was she going to tackle the subject?

How was she going to tell him that she was in serious trouble?

And how could she make him care?

She felt a shaft of pure panic and then the door opened and he strolled into the room unannounced, the sun glinting on his glossy black hair, his face hard, handsome and unsmiling.

And Kimberley realised that she was in even more trouble than she'd previously thought.

She looked like a baby deer caught in an ambush.

Without revealing any of his thoughts, Luc surveyed the slender, impossibly beautiful redhead who stood shivering and pale on the far side of his boardroom.

She looked so frightened that he almost found it possible to feel sorry for her. Except that he knew too much about her.

And if he were in her position, he'd be shaking, too.

She had one hell of a nerve, coming here!

Seven years.

He hadn't seen Kimberley Townsend for seven years and *still* she had the ability to seriously disturb his day.

Endless legs, silken hair, soft mouth and a wide, trusting smile—

For a time she'd truly had him fooled with that loving, giving, generous act that she'd perfected. Accustomed to being with women who were as sophisticated and calculating as himself, he'd been charmed and captivated by Kimberley's innocence, openness and her almost childlike honesty.

It was the first and only occasion in his adult life when he'd made a serious error of judgement.

She was a greedy little gold-digger.

He knew that now. And she knew that he knew.

So what could possibly have possessed her to throw herself in his path again?

She was either very brave or very, *very* stupid. He strolled towards her, watching her flinch and tremble and decided that she didn't look particularly brave.

Which just left stupid.

Or desperate?

Kimberley stood with her back to the wall and wondered how she could have forgotten the impact that Luciano Santoro had on women. *How could she ever have thought she could hold a man like him?*

Time had somehow dimmed the memory and the reality was enough to stun her into a temporary silence.

She was tall but he was taller. His shoulders were broad, his physique lithe and athletic and his dark, dangerous looks alone were enough to make a woman forget her own name. The truth was that, even among a race renowned for handsome men, Luc stood out from the crowd.

She stared at him with almost agonizing awareness as he strolled towards her, her eyes sliding over the glossy blue-black hair, the high cheekbones, those thick, thick lashes that shielded brooding, night-dark eyes and down to the darkened jaw of a man who seemed to embody everything it meant to be masculine. He was dressed formally in standard business attire but even the tailored perfection of his dark suit couldn't entirely disguise a nature that bordered on the very edges of civilised. Although he moved in a conventional world, Luc could never be described as 'safe' and it was that subtle hint of danger that added to his almost overwhelming appeal.

His attraction to the opposite sex was as powerful as it was predictable and she'd proved herself to be as susceptible as the rest when it came to his particular brand of lethal charm.

Feeling her heart pound against her chest, she wondered whether she'd been mad to come here.

She didn't move in his league and she never had. They played by a completely different set of rules.

And then she reminded herself firmly that she wasn't here for herself. Given the choice she never would have come near Luc again. But he was her only hope.

'Luciano.'

His eyes mocked her in that lazy, almost bored way that she used to find both aggravating and seductive. 'Very formal. You used to call me Luc.'

He spoke with a cultured male drawl that held just a hint of the dark and dangerous. The staggeringly successful international businessman mingled with the raw, rough boy from the streets.

There was enough of the hard and the tough and the ruthless in him to make her shiver. Of course he was tough and ruthless, she reasoned, trying to control the exaggerated response of her trembling body. Rumour had it that he'd dragged himself from the streets of Rio before building one of the biggest multinational businesses in the world.

'That's in the past.' And she didn't want to remember the past. Didn't want to remember the times she'd cried out his name as he'd shown her yet another way to paradise.

He raised an eyebrow and from the look in his dark eyes she knew that he was experiencing the same memories. The temperature in the room rose by several degrees and the air began to crackle and hum. 'And is that what this meeting is about? The past? You want closure? You have come to beg forgiveness and repay the money you stole?'

It was typical of him that the first thing he mentioned was the money.

For a moment her courage faltered.

'I know it was wrong to use your credit cards—' she licked her lips '—but I had a good reason—' She broke off and the carefully prepared speech that she'd rehearsed and rehearsed in her head dissolved into nothing and suddenly she couldn't think how on earth she was going to say what needed to be said.

Now, she urged herself frantically, *tell him now!*

But somehow the right words just wouldn't come.

'You *did* give me the cards—'

'One of the perks of being with me,' Luc said silkily, 'but when you spent the money, you were no longer with me. I have to congratulate you. I thought that no woman had the ability to surprise me—' he paced around her, his voice a soft, lethal drawl '—and yet you did just that. During our relationship you spent nothing. You showed no interest in my money. At the time I thought you were unique amongst your sex. I found your lack of interest in material things particularly endearing.' His tone hardened. 'Now I see that you were in fact just clever. Very clever. You held back on your spending but once you realised that the relationship was over, you showed your true colours.'

Kimberley's mouth fell open in genuine amazement. What on earth was he implying? It was *definitely* time to tell him the truth. 'I can explain where the money went—' She braced herself for the ultimate confession but he gave a dismissive shrug that indicated nothing short of total indifference.

'If there is one occupation more boring than watching a woman shop, it's hearing about it after the event.' Luc's tone was bored. 'I have absolutely no interest in the finer details of feminine indulgence.'

'Is that what you think it was?' Kimberley stared at him, aghast. 'You think I spent your money in some sort of childish female tantrum?'

'So you cheered yourself up with some new shoes and handbags.' He gave a sardonic smile. 'It is typically female behaviour. I can assure you I'm no stranger to the perceived benefits of retail therapy.'

Kimberley gasped. 'You are unbelievably insensitive!' Her voice rang with passion, anger and pain and her carefully planned speech flew out of her brain. He thought she'd been *shopping?* 'Shopping was the last thing on my mind! This was *not* retail therapy.' Her whole body trembled with indignation. 'This was *survival*. I needed the money to survive because I gave up everything to be with you. *Everything*. I gave up my job, my flat—*I moved in with you*. It was what you demanded.'

His gaze was cool. 'I don't recall a significant degree of protest on your part.'

She tilted her head back and struggled with her emotions. 'I was in love with you, Luc.' Her voice cracked and she paused for just long enough to regain control. 'I was *so* in love with you that being together was the only thing in my life that made sense. I couldn't see further than what we shared. I certainly couldn't imagine a time when we wouldn't be together.'

'Women do have a tendency to hear wedding bells when they're around me,' he observed dryly. 'In fact I would say, the larger the wallet, the louder the bells.'

'I'm not talking about marriage. I didn't *care* about marriage. I just cared about *you*.'

A muscle flickered in his lean jaw and his eyes hardened. 'Obviously you were planning for the long term.'

It took her a moment to understand the implication of his words. 'You're suggesting it was an act?' She gave a tiny laugh of disbelief and lifted a hand to her throat. Beneath the tips of her fingers she felt her pulse beating rapidly. 'You think I was pretending?'

'You were very convincing,' Luc conceded after a moment's reflection, 'but then the stakes were high, were they not? The prospect of landing a billionaire is often sufficient to produce the most commendable acting skills in a woman.'

Kimberley stared at him.

How could she ever have been foolish enough to give her love to this man? Was her judgement really that bad?

Tears clogged her throat. 'I don't consider you a prize, Luc,' she choked. 'In fact I consider you to be the biggest mistake of my life.'

'Of course you do.' He spread lean bronzed hands and gave a sympathetic smile, but his eyes were hard as flint. 'I can understand that you'd be kicking yourself for letting me slip through your fingers. All I can say is, better luck with the next guy.'

She stared into his cold, handsome face and suddenly she just wanted to sob and sob. 'You deserve to be alone in life, Luc,' she said flatly, battling not to let the emotion show on her face, 'and every woman with a grain of sense is going to let you slip right through her fingers. Given the chance, I'd drop you head first on to a tiled floor from a great height.'

He smiled an arrogant, all-male smile that reflected his unshakeable self-confidence. 'We both know you couldn't get enough of me.'

She gasped, utterly humiliated by the picture he painted. 'That was before I knew what an unfeeling, cold-hearted bastard you were!' She broke off in horror, *appalled* by her rudeness and uncharacteristic loss of control. What had come over her? 'I—I'm sorry, that was unforgivable—'

'Don't apologise for showing your true colours.' Far from being offended, he looked mildly amused. 'Believe it or not,

I prefer honesty in a woman. It saves all sorts of misunderstanding.'

She lifted a hand to her forehead in an attempt to relieve the ache between her temples.

It had been so hard for her to come here. So hard to brace herself to tell him the things that he needed to know. And so far none of it had gone as planned.

She had things that had to be said and she just didn't know how to say them. Instead of talking about the present, they were back in the past and that was the one place she didn't want to be. Unless she could use the past to remind him of what they'd once shared—

'You cared, Luc,' she said softly, her hands dropping to her sides in a helpless gesture. 'I *know* you cared. I felt it.'

She appealed to the man that she'd once believed him to be.

'I was very turned on by the fact I was your first lover,' he agreed in a smooth tone. 'In fact I was totally knocked out by the novelty of the experience. Naturally I was keen for you to enjoy it too. You were very shy and it was in both our interests for you to be relaxed. I did what needed to be done and said what needed to be said.'

Her cheeks flamed with embarrassment. In other words he was so experienced with women that he knew exactly which buttons to press. In her case he'd sensed that she needed closeness and affection. *It hadn't meant anything to him.*

'So you're saying it was all an act?' The pain inside her blossomed. 'Being loving and gentle was just another of your many seduction methods?'

He shrugged as if he could see no problem with that. 'I didn't hear you complaining.'

She closed her eyes. How could she have been so gullible? Yes, she'd been a virgin but that was no excuse for bald stupidity. Sixteen years of living with a man like her father should have taught her everything she needed to know about men. He'd moved from one woman to another, never making a commitment, never giving anything. Just using. Using and discarding. Her mother had walked out just after Kimberley's fourth birthday and from that moment on she had a series of 'Aunties', women who came into her father's life and then left with a volley of shouts and jealous accusations. Kimberley had promised herself that she was never, *ever* going to let a man treat her the way her father treated women. She was going to find one man and she was going to love him.

And then she'd met Luc and for a short, crazy period of time she'd thought he was that man. She'd ignored his reputation with women, ignored any similarities to her father, ignored her promise to herself.

She'd broken all her own rules.

And she'd paid the price.

'What did I ever do to make you treat me so cruelly?' Suddenly she needed to understand. Wanted to know what had gone wrong—how she could have made such an enormous mistake. 'Why did you need other women?'

'I've never been a one woman kind of guy,' he admitted without a trace of apology or regret, 'and you're all pretty much the same, as you went on to prove with your truly awesome spending spree.'

She flinched. This would be a perfect time to confess. To tell him exactly *why* she'd needed the money so badly. She took a deep breath and braced herself for the truth. 'I spent your money because I needed it for something very important,' she said hesitantly, 'and before I tell you exactly what, I want you to know that I *did* try and talk to you at the time but you wouldn't see me, and—'

'Is this conversation going anywhere?' He glanced at his watch in a gesture of supreme boredom. 'I've already told you that your spending habits don't interest me. And if you'd needed funds then maybe you should have tapped your other lover for the cash.'

She gasped. 'I didn't *have* other lovers. You *know* I didn't.'

There'd only ever been him. Just him.

'I don't know anything of the kind.' His eyes hardened. 'On two occasions I returned home to be told that you were "out".'

'Because I was tired of lying in our bed waiting for you to come home from some other woman's arms!' She exploded with exasperation, determined to defend herself. 'Yes, I went out! And you just couldn't stand that, could you? And why not? Because you *always* have to be the one in control.'

'It wasn't about control.' His gaze simmered, dark with all the volatility of his exotic heritage. 'You didn't need to leave. You were *mine*.'

And he thought that wasn't about control?

'You make me sound like a possession!' Her voice rang with pain and frustration. She was *trying* to say what needed to be said but each time she tried to talk about the present they seemed to end up back in the past. 'You treat every woman like a possession! To be used and discarded when you're had enough! That's why our relationship never would have worked. You're ruthless, self-seeking and totally without morals or thought for other people. You expected me to lie there and wait for you to finish partying and come home!'

'Instead of which, you decided to expand your sexual horizons,' he said coldly and she resisted the temptation to leap at him and claw at his handsome face.

How could such an intelligent, successful man be so dense about women? He couldn't see past the end of his nose.

'You went out, so I went out.' Wisps of hair floated across her face and she brushed them away with an impatient hand. 'What was I supposed to do when you weren't there?'

'You were supposed to get some rest,' he delivered in silky tones, 'and wait for me to come home.'

Neanderthal man. She was expected to wait in the cave for the hunter to return.

Exasperated beyond belief, she resisted the temptation to walk out and slam the door. 'This is the twenty-first century, Luc! Women vote. They run companies. They decide their own social lives.'

'And they cheat on their partners.' He gave a sardonic lift of his brows. 'Progress, indeed.'

'I did *not* cheat!' She stared at him in outrage, wondering how such an intelligent man could be so dense when it came to relationships. *She'd loved him so much.* 'You were the one photographed in a restaurant with another woman. Clearly I wasn't enough for you.' She gave a casual shrug and tried to keep the pain out of her voice. 'Naturally I assumed that if you were out seeing other people then I could do the same. But I did not cheat!'

'I don't want the details.'

They were closing in on each other. A step here, a slight movement there.

'Well, perhaps you should, instead of jumping to conclusions,' she suggested shakily, 'and if a sin was committed then it was yours, Luc. I was eighteen years old and yet you seduced me without even a flicker of conscience. And then you moved on without a flicker of conscience. Tell me—did you give it any thought? Before you took my virginity and wrecked my life, *did you give it any thought?*'

His dark gaze swept over her with naked incredulity. 'You have been back in my life for five minutes and already you are snapping and snarling and hurling accusations. You were only too willing to be seduced, my flame-haired temptress, but if you've forgotten that fact then I'm happy to jog your memory.' Without warning he closed lean brown fingers around her wrist and jerked her hard against him. The connection was immediate and powerful.

'That first night, in the back of my car, when you wrapped that amazing body of yours around mine—' his voice was a low, dangerous purr and the warmth of his breath teased her mouth '—was that not an invitation?'

The air around them crackled and sparked with tension.

She tugged at her wrist but he held her easily and she remembered just how much she'd loved that about him. His strength. His vibrant, undiluted masculinity. In fact she'd positively relished the differences between them. His dark male power to her feminine softness. *Her good to his very, very bad.*

He was *so* strong and she'd always felt incredibly safe when she was with him. At the beginning that had been part of the attraction. Particularly that first night, as he'd just reminded her. 'I'd been attacked. I was frightened—'

And he'd rescued her. Using street fighting skills that didn't go with the sleek dinner jacket he'd been wearing, he'd taken on six men and had extracted her with apparently very little damage to himself. As a tactic designed to impress a woman, it had proved a winner.

'So you wanted comfort.' His grip on her wrist tightened. 'So when you slid on to my lap and begged me to kiss you, was that not an invitation? Or was that comfort too?'

Hot colour of mortification flooded her smooth cheeks. 'I don't know what happened to me that night—'

She'd taken one look at him and suddenly believed in fairy tales. Knights. Dragons. Maidens in distress. *He was the one.* Or so she'd thought—

'You discovered your true self,' he said roughly. 'That's what happened. So don't accuse me of seducing you when we both know that I only took what you freely offered. You were hot for me and you stayed hot—'

'*I was innocent—*'

His breath warmed her mouth and he gave a slow, sexy smile that made her heart thud hard against her chest. 'You were desperate.'

He was going to kiss her.

She recognised the signs, saw the darkening of his eyes and the lowering of those thick, thick lashes as his heated gaze swept her flushed face.

The tension throbbed and pulsed between them and then suddenly he released her with a soft curse and took a step backwards.

'So why are you here?' His tone was suddenly icy cold, and there was anger in the glint of his dark eyes. 'You wish to reminisce? You are hoping for a repeat performance, perhaps? If so, you should probably know that women only get one chance in my bed and you blew it.'

A repeat performance?

Erotic memories flashed through her brain and she took a step backwards, as if to escape from them. 'Let's get this straight.' Despite all her best efforts, her voice shook slightly. '*Nothing* would induce me to climb back into your bed, Luc. Nothing. That was one life experience I have no intention of repeating. Ever. I'm not that stupid.'

He stilled and a look of masculine speculation flickered across his handsome face. 'Is that a fact?'

Too late she realised that a man like Luc would probably consider that a challenge. And he was a man who loved a challenge.

She looked at him helplessly, wondering how on earth the conversation had developed into this. For some reason they were right back where they'd left off seven years before and it wasn't what she'd planned.

She'd intended to be cool and businesslike and to avoid anything remotely personal. Instead of which, their verbal exchange had so far been entirely personal.

And still she hadn't told him what she needed to tell him. Still she hadn't said what needed to be said.

He prowled around her slowly and a slightly mocking smile touched his firm mouth. 'Still so much passion, Kimberley, and still trying to hold it in check and pretend it doesn't exist. That it isn't a part of you and yet how could your nature be anything else?' He brushed a hand over her hair with a mocking smile. 'Never get involved with a woman who has hair the colour of dragon's breath.'

Kimberley lifted her chin and her green eyes flashed. 'And never get involved with a man who has an ego the size of Brazil.'

He laughed. 'Ours was never the most tranquil of relationships, was it *meu amorzinho?*'

Meu amorzinho. He'd always called her that and she'd loved hearing him speak in his native language. It had seemed so much more exotic than the English translation, 'my little love'.

His unexpected laughter released some of the throbbing tension in the room and she felt the colour flood into her face as she remembered, too late, that she'd promised herself she wasn't going to fight with him. She couldn't afford to fight with him. 'We both need to forget the past.' Determined not to let him unsettle her, she took a deep breath and tried to find the tranquillity that usually came naturally to her. 'Both of us have moved on. I'm not the same person any more.'

'You're exactly the same person, Kimberley.' He strolled around her, like a jungle animal assessing its prey. 'Inside, people never really change. It's just the packaging that's different. The way they present themselves to the world.'

Before she could guess his intention, he lifted a lean bronze hand and in a deft, skilful movement removed the clip from her hair.

She gasped a protest and clutched at the fiery mass that tumbled over her shoulders. 'What do you think you're doing?'

'Altering the packaging. Reminding you who you really are under the costume you're wearing.' His burning gaze slid lazily down her body. 'You come in here, suitably dressed to teach a class of schoolchildren or sort books in a library, that hot red hair all twisted away and tamed. On the outside you are all buttoned up and locked away, yet we both know what sort of person you are on the inside.' His dark eyes fixed on hers and his voice was rich and seductive. 'Passionate. Wild.'

His tongue rolled over the words, his accent more pronounced than usual, and she felt her stomach flip over and her knees weaken.

'You're wrong! That's not who I am! You have no idea who I am.' Despite her promise to herself that she'd remain cool, she couldn't hold back the emotion. 'Did you really think I'd be the same pathetic little girl you seduced all those years ago? Do you really think I haven't changed?'

Despite her heated denials, she felt a flash of sexual awareness that appalled her and she squashed it down with grim determination.

She wasn't going to let him do this to her again. She wasn't going to feel anything.

She'd come here to tell him something she should have told him seven years ago, not to resurrect feelings that she'd taken years to bury.

'You weren't pathetic and neither,' he said softly, touching a curl of fiery red hair, 'did I seduce you, determined though you seem to be to believe that. Our passion was as mutual as it was hot, *meu amorzinho*. You were with me all the way.' He said the words 'all the way' with a smooth, erotic emphasis that started a slow burn deep within her pelvis. 'The only difference between us was that you were ashamed of how you felt. I assumed that maturity would allow you to embrace your passionate nature instead of rejecting it.'

To her horror she felt her body start to melt and her breath-

ing grow shallow and she shrank away from him, desperate
to stop the reaction.

How?

How, after all these years and all the thinking time she'd
had, could she still react to this man?

Did she never learn?

And then she remembered that she *had* learned. The hard
way. And it didn't matter how her body responded to this man,
this time her brain was in charge. She was older and more experienced and well able to ignore the insidious curl of sexual
desire deep in her pelvis.

'This isn't what I came here for.' She lifted a hand to her
hair and smoothed it away from her face. 'What happened between you and me isn't important.'

'So you keep saying. So what *is* important enough to bring
you all the way back to Rio de Janeiro when you left and
swore never to return, I wonder? Our golden beaches? Our
dramatic mountains?' His rich accent rolled over the words.
'The addictive beat of the samba? I recall that evening that
we danced on my terrace…'

He flicked memories in front of her like a slide show and
she looked away for a moment, forcing herself to focus on
something bland and inanimate, trying to dilute the disturbing images in her head. The chair drew the full force of her
gaze while she composed herself and plucked up the courage
to say what she had to say.

'I want us to stop talking about the past.' She paused for a
moment and felt her knees turn to liquid. It was now. It had
to be now. 'I'm here because—' Her voice cracked and she
licked dry lips and tried again. 'I'm trying to tell you—w-we
had a son together, Luc, and he's now six years old.' Her heart
pounded and her body trembled. 'He's six years old and his
life is in danger. I'm here because I need your help. I've no
one else to turn to.'

CHAPTER TWO

How could silence seem so loud?

Was he ever going to speak?

Relief that she'd finally told him mingled with apprehension. What was he going to say? How was he going to react to the sudden discovery that he was a father?

'Well, that's inventive.' His tone was flat and he sprawled in the nearest chair, his eyes veiled as he watched her, always the one in control, always the one calling the shots. 'You certainly know how to keep a guy on his toes. I never know what you're going to come up with next.'

Kimberley blinked, totally taken aback.

He didn't believe her?

She'd prepared herself for anger and recrimination. She'd braced herself to be on the receiving end of his hot Brazilian temper. She'd been prepared to explain why she hadn't told him seven years before. But it hadn't once crossed her mind that he might not believe her.

'You seriously think I'd joke about something like that?'

He gave a casual shrug. 'I admit it's in pretty poor taste, but some women will stoop to just about anything to get a man to fork out. And I presume that's what you want? More money?'

It was exactly what she wanted but not for any of the reasons he seemed to be implying.

Her mouth opened and shut and she swallowed hard, totally out of her depth. She hadn't even entertained the possibility that he wouldn't believe her and she honestly didn't know what to say next. She'd geared herself up for this moment and it wasn't going according to her script.

'*Why* wouldn't you believe me?'

'Possibly because women don't suddenly turn up after seven years of silence and announce that they're pregnant.'

'I didn't say I was p-pregnant,' she stammered, appalled and frustrated that he refused to take her seriously. 'I told you, he's *six*. He was born precisely forty weeks after we had— after you—' She broke off, blushing furiously, and his gaze dropped to her mouth, lingered and then lifted again.

'After I had my wicked way with you? You're so repressed you can't even bring yourself to say the word "sex".' His dark eyes mocked her gently and she bit her lip, wishing she was more sophisticated—better equipped to deal with this sort of situation. Verbal sparring wasn't her forte and yet she was dealing with a master.

He'd wronged her and yet suddenly she felt as though she should be apologising. 'You're probably wondering why I didn't tell you this before—'

'The thought had crossed my mind.'

'You threw me out, Luc,' she reminded him in a shaky voice, 'and you refused to see me or take my calls. You treated me *abominably*.'

'Relationships end every day of the week,' he drawled in a tone of total indifference. 'Stop being so dramatic.'

'*I was pregnant!*' She rose to her feet, shaking with emotion, goaded into action by his total lack of remorse. 'I decided that you ought to know about your child. I tried to tell you so many times but you cut me out of your life. *And you hurt me.* You hurt me so badly that I decided that no child of mine was going to have you as a father. And *that's* why I didn't tell you.' She broke off, waiting for an angry reaction on his part, waiting for him to storm and rant that she hadn't told him sooner.

Instead he raised an eyebrow expectantly. 'Seven years and this is the best you can come up with?'

She stared at him blankly, unable to comprehend his callous indifference. 'Do you think I made that decision lightly? *Have you any idea what making a decision like that does to a person?* I felt screwed up with guilt, Luc! I was depriving my son of a father and I knew that one day I'd have to answer to him for that.' She broke off and dragged a shuddering breath into her starving lungs. 'I have felt guilty every single day for the last seven years. *Every single day.*'

'Yes, well, that's another woman thing—guilt,' Luc said helpfully, 'and I suppose that all this *guilt* suddenly overwhelmed you and that's why you've suddenly decided to share your joyous news with me?'

She shook her head. 'I can't *believe* you're behaving like this. Do you *know* how hard it was for me to come here today? *Have you any idea?'* He was even more unfeeling than she'd believed possible. How could she feel guilt? She should be *proud* that she'd protected her son from this man. But the time for protection had passed and, unfortunately for everyone, she now needed his help. She couldn't afford the luxury of cutting him out of her life. 'What do I have to do to prove that I'm telling the truth?'

Luc turned his head and glanced towards the door expectantly. 'Produce him.' He lifted broad shoulders in a careless shrug. 'That should do the trick.'

She looked at him in disbelief. 'You seriously think I'd drag a six-year-old all the way to Brazil to meet a man who doesn't even know he's a father? This is a huge thing, Luc. We need to discuss how we're going to handle it. How we're going to tell him. It needs to be a joint decision.'

There was a sardonic gleam in his dark eyes. 'Well, that's going to be a problem, isn't it? I don't do joint decisions. Never have, never will. I'm unilateral all the way, *meu amorzinho*. But in this case it really doesn't matter because we both know that this so called "son" of yours, oh, sorry—' he corrected himself with an apologetic smile and a lift of his hand '—I should say son of *"ours"*, shouldn't I?—is a figment of your greedy, money-grabbing imagination. So it would be impossible for you to produce him. Unless you hired someone to play the part. Have you?'

Kimberley gaped at him.

He was an utter bastard!

How could she have forgotten just how cold and unfeeling he was? What a low opinion of women he had? How could she have thought, even for a moment, that she'd made a mistake in not persisting in her attempts to tell him that she was expecting his child? At the time she'd decided that she could never expose a child of hers to a man like him and, listening to him now, she knew that it had *definitely* been the right decision.

People had criticised her behind her back, she knew that, but they were people who came from safe, loving homes—homes where the father came home at night and cared about what happened to his family.

Luc wasn't like that. Luc didn't care about anything or anyone except himself.

He was *just* like her father and she knew only too well what it was like to grow up with a parent like that. She'd been right to protect her child from him and if it hadn't been for her current crisis she would have continued to keep Luc out of his life.

But fate had intervened and she'd decided that she had no choice but to tell him. He *had* to help her. He *had* to take some responsibility, however distasteful he found the prospect of parenthood.

But at the moment he didn't even believe that his son existed—

He seemed to think that their child was some sort of figment of her greedy imagination.

She sank on to the nearest chair, bemused and sickened by his less than flattering assessment of her. 'Why do you have such a low opinion of me?'

'Well, let's see—' he gave a patient smile, as if he was dealing with someone very, *very* stupid '—it could have something to do with the volume of money you spent after we broke up. Or the fact that you're now stooping to depths previously unheard of in order to sue me for maintenance. *Not* the actions of someone destined for sainthood, wouldn't you agree?'

She stared at him blankly. Her mind didn't work along the same lines as his and she was struggling to keep up. 'I'm not suing you for maintenance.'

He gave an impatient frown. 'You want me to pay money for the child.'

She licked her lips. 'Yes, but not to *me* and it's nothing to do with maintenance. I can support our son. I took the money from you because I was pregnant, alone and very scared and I couldn't think how I could possibly bring a child into the world when I didn't even have somewhere to live. I used your money to buy a small flat. If I hadn't done that I would have had to find a job and put the baby into a nursery, and I wanted to care for him myself. And I bought a few essentials.' She gave a tiny frown, momentarily distracted. 'I had no idea how many things a baby needed. I bought a cot and a pushchair, bedding, nappies. I didn't use any of the money on myself. I *know* that technically it was stealing, but I didn't know what else to do so I told myself it was maintenance. If I'd chased you through the courts you would have had to pay a lot more to support Rio.'

One dark eyebrow swooped upwards. *'Rio?'*

She blushed. 'I chose to name him after the city where he was conceived.'

'How quaint.' Luc's tone was a deep, dark drawl loaded with undertones of menace. 'So if I've already paid for the pushchair and the nappies, what else is there? He needs a new school coat, perhaps? His feet have grown and his shoes no longer fit?'

He still didn't believe her.

'Last week I received a kidnap threat.' Her voice shook as she said the words. Perhaps the truth would shake him out of his infuriating cool. 'Someone out there knows about our son. They know you're a father. And they're threatening Rio's life.'

There was a long silence while he watched her, his dark eyes fixed on her pale face.

They were sitting too close to each other. *Much too close.*

Her knee brushed against his and she felt the insidious warmth of awareness spread through her body. Against her will, her eyes slid to the silken dark hairs visible on his wrist and then rested on his strong fingers. *Those long, clever fingers—*

Her body flooded with heat as she remembered how those fingers had introduced her to intimacies that she'd never before imagined and she shifted slightly in her chair. His eyes detected the movement. Instantly his gaze trapped hers and the temperature in the room rose still further.

'Show me the letter.'

Did she imagine the sudden rough tone to his voice? Relieved that she could finally meet one of his demands, she delved into her bag and dragged out the offending letter, dropping it on the table next to him as if it might bite her.

He extended a hand and lifted the letter, no visible sense of urgency apparent in his movements. He flipped it open and read it, his handsome face inscrutable.

'Interesting.' He dropped the letter back on the table. 'So I'm expected to shell out five million dollars and then everyone lives happily ever after? Have I got that right?'

She stared at him, stunned, more than a little taken aback that he didn't seem more concerned for the welfare of his son. Still, at least now he'd seen the evidence, he'd know she was telling the truth.

'Do you think paying is the wrong approach? You think we should go to the police?' She looked at him anxiously and rubbed her fingers across her forehead, trying to ease the pain that pulsed behind her temples. She'd gone over and over it in her head so many times, trying to do the right thing. 'I have thought about it, obviously, but you can see from the letter what he threatened to do if I spoke to the police. I know everyone always says you shouldn't pay blackmailers, but that's very easy to say when it isn't your child in danger and—' her voice cracked '—and I can't play games with his life, Luc. He's everything I have.'

She looked at the strong, hard lines of Luc's face and suddenly wanted him to step in and save her the way he'd saved her that first night they'd met. He was hard and ruthless and he had powerful connections and she knew instinctively that he would be able to handle this situation if he chose to. He could make it go away.

'I think involving the police would *not* be a good idea,' he assured her, rising to his feet in a lithe, athletic movement and pacing across the office to the window. 'Police in any country don't generally appreciate having their time wasted.'

Her eyes widened. 'But why would this waste their time?'

He shot her an impatient look. 'Because we both know that this is all part of your elaborate plan to extract more money from me. I suppose I should just be grateful it took you seven years to work your way through the last lot.' His voice was harsh and contemptuous. 'It was a master stroke suggesting we contact the police because it does add credibility to the situation, but we both know that would have proved somewhat embarrassing if they'd agreed to be involved.'

She stared at him in stunned silence. 'You still think I'm making this whole situation up, don't you?'

'Look at it from my point of view,' he advised silkily. 'You turn up after seven years, demanding money to help a child I know nothing about and whose existence you cannot prove. If he's my child, why didn't you tell me you were pregnant seven years ago?'

'I've already explained!' She ran a hand over the back of her neck to relieve the tension. 'Over and over again I rang and came to your office and you refused to see me. You wouldn't even *talk* to me.'

He'd cut her dead and she'd thought she'd die from the pain. She'd missed him *so* much.

'Our relationship was over and talking about it after the event isn't my forte.' Luc gave a careless shrug. 'Talking is something else that's more of a woman thing than a man thing. A bit like guilt, I suppose.'

'Well, just because you're totally lacking in communication skills, don't blame me now for the fact you weren't told about your child!' Her emotions rumbled like a volcano on the point of eruption. 'I *tried* to tell you, but your listening skills need serious attention.'

His eyes hardened. 'It's a funny thing, but I always find that I become slightly hard of hearing when people are begging me for money.'

She stared at him helplessly. 'He's your *son*—'

He held out a hand. 'So show me a photograph.'

'Sorry?'

'If he exists, then at least show me a photograph.'

She felt as though she was on the witness stand being questioned by a particularly nasty prosecutor. 'I—I don't have one with me. I was in a panic and I didn't think to bring one.' *But she should have.* Should have known Luc would ask to at least see a picture of his child. 'I wasn't expecting to have to prove his existence, so no, I don't have a photograph.'

One dark eyebrow swooped upwards and his hand fell to his side. 'What a loving mother you must be.' His tone was dangerously soft. 'You don't even carry a photograph of your own child.'

She exploded with exasperation. 'I don't *need* to carry a photograph of him because I'm with him virtually every minute of every day and have been since he was born! I used your money to buy a little flat so that I could stay at home and look after him. And now he's older I work from home so that I don't miss a single minute of being with him. I don't need photographs! I have the real thing!'

He inclined his head and a ghost of a smile touched his firm mouth. 'Good answer.'

She shook her head slowly, helpless to know what to do to convince him. 'You think I'm making all this up just to get money for myself?'

'Frankly?' The smile vanished. 'I think you're a greedy, money-grabbing bitch who wants five million dollars and is prepared to go to most distasteful lengths to achieve that goal.' His eyes scanned her face. 'And you can abandon the wounded look—it's less convincing once you've already ripped a guy off big time.'

Her mouth fell open and her body chilled with shock. '*Why* would you think that about me?'

'Because I already know you're greedy,' he said helpfully, checking his watch. 'And now you'll have to excuse me because I have a Japanese delegation waiting in another meeting room who are equally eager to drain my bank account. If they're even half as inventive as you've been then I'm in for an interesting afternoon.'

She stared at him in horrified disbelief.

Was that it?

Was he really going to walk out on her?

She knew instinctively that if he left the room now, she wouldn't see him again. Gaining access to Luciano Santoro was an honour extended only to a privileged few and she sensed that she was on borrowed time.

'No!' She stood up quickly and her voice rang with panic. Her feelings didn't matter any more. Nothing mattered except the safety of her son. 'You can't just send me away! I'm telling the truth and I'll prove it if I have to. I can get Rio on the phone, I can arrange for you to talk to the school, I'll do anything, *absolutely anything,* but you have to give me the money. I'm *begging* you, Luc. *Please* lend me the money. I'll pay you back somehow, but if you don't give it to me I don't know what else to do. I don't know where else to turn—'

She broke off, her slim shoulders drooped as the fight drained out of her, and she slumped into a chair.

He wasn't going to help her. The responsibility of being a single parent had always felt enormous, but never more so than now, when her child's safety was threatened.

She wanted to lean on someone. She wanted to share the burden.

Luc stilled and his dark eyes narrowed. 'For five million dollars you'd do *absolutely anything*?'

There was something in his tone that made her uneasy but she didn't hesitate. 'I'm a mother and what mother wouldn't agree to anything if it meant keeping her child safe?'

'Well, that's a very interesting offer.' His eyes scanned her face thoughtfully. 'I'll think about it.'

She bit her lip and clasped her hands in her lap. 'I need an answer quickly.'

'This is Brazil, *meu amorzinho,*' he reminded gently,

stretching lean muscular legs out in front of him, 'and you of all people should know that we don't do anything quickly.'

She caught her breath, trapped by the burning heat in his eyes and the tense, pulsing atmosphere in the room. All at once she was transported back to long, lazy afternoons making love on his bed, in the swimming pool—afternoons that had stretched into evenings that had stretched into mornings.

She swallowed as she remembered the slow, throbbing, intense heat of those days.

No, Brazilians certainly didn't rush anything.

'The deadline is tomorrow night.'

His eyes gleamed. 'So many shoes, so little time. You think I will just give you the money and let you go? Is that what you think?'

She swallowed, hypnotised by the look in his eyes. 'Luc—'

'Let's look at the facts, shall we?' Lean bronzed fingers beat a slow, menacing rhythm on the glass table. 'You clearly hold me responsible for seducing you seven years ago. You come into my office ignoring the past as though it is a vile disease that you could catch again if you stay close to me for long enough.' His gaze swept over her. 'Everything about you is buttoned up. You are wearing your clothes like armour, protecting yourself and the truth is—' he leaned towards her, his dark eyes mocking '—you are afraid of those things I made you feel, are you not? You are afraid of your own response to me. That is why you deny your feelings. It is so much easier to pretend that they don't exist.'

The breath she'd been about to take lodged in her throat. 'I don't feel anything—'

He gave a lethal smile. 'You forget, *minha docura*, that I was once intimately acquainted with every delicious inch of you. I know the signs. I recognise that flush on your cheeks, I recognise the way your eyes glaze and your lips part just before you beg me to kiss you.'

Completely unsettled by his words, Kimberley rose to her feet so quickly she almost knocked the chair over. 'You're insufferably arrogant!'

Her heart was pounding heavily and everything about her whole body suddenly felt warm and tingly.

'I'm honest,' he drawled, swivelling in his seat so that he could survey her from under slightly lowered lids, 'which is more than you have ever been, I suspect. It is so much easier to blame me, is it not, than to accept responsibility yourself? Why is it that you find sex so shameful, I wonder?'

She couldn't catch her breath properly. 'Because sex should be part of a loving relationship,' she blurted out before she could stop herself and he gave a smile that was totally male.

'If you believe that then clearly maturity has added nothing to your ability to face facts.'

Tears pricked her eyes. '*Why* are you so cynical?'

He shrugged. 'I am realistic and, like most men, I don't need the pretence of love to justify enjoying good sex.'

How had she ever allowed herself to become involved with this man?

They were just *so* different. 'I—I hate you—'

'You don't hate me—' his relaxed pose was in complete contrast to her rising tension ' but I know you *think* you do, which makes this whole situation more intriguing by the minute. You would so much rather be anywhere else but here. Which makes your greed all the more deplorable. You must want money very badly to risk walking into the dragon's den.'

'I've told you why I need the money and this situation has nothing to do with *us*—we've both moved on.' Her fingers curled into her palms. 'I know you're not still interested in me, any more than I'm still interested in you.'

'Is that a fact?' His voice was a deep, dark drawl and he lounged in his seat with careless ease, contemplating her with lazy amusement. 'And what if you're wrong? What if I *am* still interested in you?'

Her mouth dried. 'You're being ridiculous.'

'A word of advice—' His voice was suddenly soft and his eyes glittered, dark and dangerous. 'When you're trying to relieve someone of an indecent sum of money, don't accuse them of being ridiculous.'

She swallowed. How could she ever have thought she was a match for this man? She was a different person around him. Her brain didn't move and her tongue didn't form the right words.

She should never have come, she thought helplessly. 'If you won't lend me the money then there's no more to be said.'

She'd failed.

Panic threatened to choke her and she curled her fingers into her palms and walked towards the door.

'Walk out of that door and you won't be allowed back in,' he informed her in silky tones. 'Come back and sit down.'

Would he be ordering her to sit down if he had no intention of lending her the money?

Hope mingled with caution and she turned, her hand on the door handle and her heart in her mouth.

'I said, sit down.' His strong face was expressionless and, with barely any hesitation, she did as he ordered and then immediately hated herself for being that predictable. For doing exactly what he said.

Wasn't that what her whole life had been like for that one month they'd spent together? He'd commanded and she'd obeyed, too much in love and in lust to even think of resisting. Completely overwhelmed by him in every way. And here she was, seven years on, in his company for less than an hour and still obeying his every command.

Well, it wasn't going to happen that way again.

She wasn't that person any more, and being in the same room as him didn't make her that person.

Her expression was defiant as she looked at him. 'It's a simple question, Luc. Yes or no. It doesn't matter whether I sit or stand and it doesn't matter whether I leave the room. All the information you need is in that letter in front of you.'

The letter he clearly thought was a fake.

She watched in despair as he gave a casual shrug and pushed it away from him in a gesture of total indifference. 'I have no interest in the letter or in your stories about phantom pregnancies. What *does* interest me, *meu amorzinho*, is the fact that you came to me.'

She froze. 'I already told you, I—'

'I heard—' he interrupted her gently, 'you came to me to tell me you would do *absolutely anything* for five million dollars and now I simply have to decide exactly what form *absolutely anything* is going to take. When I've worked it out, you'll be the first to know.'

CHAPTER THREE

BACK in her hotel room, Kimberley dragged off the jacket of her suit and dropped on to the bed, fighting off tears of frustration and anxiety.

She'd blown it. She'd totally blown it.

She'd planned to be calm and rational, to tell him the facts and explain the reasons for having kept Rio's birth a secret from him for so long. But from the moment he'd walked into the room her plans had flown out of the window.

She'd been catapulted back into the past.

And she had less than twenty-four hours before the deadline came and went. Less than twenty-four hours in which to persuade a man with no morals or human decency to deposit five million dollars into the blackmailer's bank account.

The blackmailer he didn't even believe existed.

She took several deep breaths, struggling to hold herself together emotionally. It had been the hardest thing in the world to leave her child at this point in time, when all her instincts as a mother told her to keep him close. But she had known that to bring him on this trip would have been to expose him to even greater danger. And she'd hoped that she would only be in Rio de Janeiro for two days at the most. And after that—

She closed her eyes briefly and took a deep breath. She

hadn't dared think further than this meeting. Hadn't dared think what would happen if Luc refused to lend her the money.

Even now, with the letter still lurking in her handbag, she couldn't quite believe that this was happening. Couldn't believe that someone, somewhere, had discovered the truth about her child's parentage. She'd been so careful *and yet somehow they knew.*

And she'd left her son with the only person in the world that she trusted. The man who was a father figure to him.

As if by telepathy the phone in her bag rang and she answered it swiftly.

'Is he all right?'

Jason's voice came back, reassuringly familiar. 'He's fine. Stop fussing.' They'd agreed not to discuss any details on the phone. 'How are you? Any luck your end?'

Kimberley felt the panic rise again. 'Not yet.' She couldn't bring herself to tell Jason that Luc didn't believe her. Part of her was still hoping for a miracle.

'But Luc agreed to see you this time? You met with him?'

Kimberley's fingers tightened on the phone. 'Oh, yes.' And her whole body was still humming and tingling as a result of that encounter. 'But he won't give me an answer. He's playing games.'

'Did he fall on bended knee and beg your forgiveness for treating you so shoddily?'

Kimberley tipped her head back and struggled with tears as she recalled every detail of their explosive meeting. 'Not exactly—'

'I don't suppose "sorry" is in his vocabulary.' Jason gave a short laugh that was distinctly lacking in humour. 'Hang in there. If he doesn't come banging on your door in the next hour then he isn't the man I think he is.'

Banging on her door? Why would he do that?

Kimberley gave a sigh. She knew only too well that Luc Santoro didn't go round banging on women's doors. Usually they fell at his feet and he just scooped them out of his path and dropped them in his bed until he'd had enough of them.

'I wish I had your confidence. What if he refuses?'

'He won't refuse. Have courage.' Jason's voice was firm. 'But I still think we should talk to the police.'

'No!' She sat bolt upright on the bed and swept her tangled hair out of her eyes. *'Not* the police. You saw the note. You *know* what that man threatened to do—'

'All right. But if you change your mind—'

'I won't change my mind.' She wouldn't do anything that would jeopardize the safety of her child. 'All I want is to deposit the money in his account as he instructed. I don't want to do anything that might upset him or give him reason to hurt Rio.'

Limp with the heat and exhaustion, Kimberley snapped the phone shut and lay back on the bed and closed her eyes. For a moment she questioned her decision to stay in this small hotel with no air-conditioning in a slightly dubious part of Rio de Janeiro. At the time it had seemed the right thing to do because she didn't want to squander money, but now, with the perspiration prickling her skin and her head throbbing, she wished she'd chosen somewhere else. She was hot, she was miserable and she hadn't eaten or slept since the letter had arrived two days previously.

Instead she'd spent the time pacing the floor of her London flat, planning strategy with Jason. It had been hard to act as if nothing was wrong in front of her little boy. Even harder to board a plane to Rio de Janeiro without him, because apart from the time he spent at school or playing with friends, they were hardly ever apart.

She'd stayed at home when he was little and, with the help of Jason, a top fashion photographer who she'd met when she was modelling, she'd started working from home, selling her own designs of jewellery. She'd managed to fit her working hours around caring for her new baby and she'd worked hard to push all thoughts and memories of Luc Santoro out of her system.

And she'd dealt with the enormous guilt by telling herself that there were some men who just weren't cut out to be fathers and Luc was definitely one of them. He was a man like her father—a man who shifted his attention from one woman to the next without any thought of commitment—and she vowed that no child of hers was ever going to experience the utter misery and chronic insecurity that she'd suffered as a child.

Finding the heat suddenly intolerable, Kimberley sprang to her feet and stripped off the rest of her clothes before padding barefoot into the tiny bathroom in an attempt to seek relief from the unrelenting humidity.

The shower could barely be described as such, but it was sufficient to cool her heated flesh and she washed and dried herself and then slid into clean underwear and collapsed back on to the bed, wishing that the ceiling fan worked.

'Presumably this is all part of your plan to gain the sympathy vote, staying in a hotel with no air-conditioning in a part of town that even the police avoid.' His deep, dark drawl came from the doorway and she gave a gasp of shock and sprang off the bed.

She hadn't even heard the door open.

'You can't just walk in here!' She made a grab for her robe and dragged it around herself, self-conscious and just horrified that he'd caught her in such a vulnerable state. Her hair was hanging in dark, damp coils down her back and she wasn't wearing any make-up. She felt completely unprepared for a confrontation with a man like him. 'You should have knocked!'

'You should have locked the door.' He strolled into the room and closed the door firmly behind him, turning the key with a smooth, deliberate movement. 'In this part of town, you can't be too careful.'

Hands shaking, she tied the robe at the waist, still glaring at him. 'What are you doing here?'

'I was under the impression that you wanted an urgent answer to your request for funds.' He strolled across the cramped, airless room and stared out of the smeared window into the grimy, litter infested street below. His broad shoulders all but obliterated the light in the room and she couldn't see his face. 'If your finances are in this bad a state, perhaps you ought to be asking me for more than five million.'

She didn't answer. She couldn't. She could hardly breathe, trapped in this tiny, airless room with Luc Santoro, who dominated every inch of available space with his powerful body. He was still wearing the sleek business suit and the jacket moulded to his shoulders, hinting at masculine strength and power. His glossy hair brushed the collar of his white silk shirt, just on the edges of what would be considered respectable in the cut-throat world of corporate finance. His hard jaw betrayed the tell-tale signs of dark stubble and at that precise moment, even dressed in the suit, he looked more bandit than businessman.

He was wickedly, dangerously attractive and with a rush of horror she felt her nipples harden and push against the soft fabric of her robe.

Mortified by her own reaction, she wrapped her arms around her waist and tried to remind herself that none of that mattered. It didn't matter how her body reacted to this man. This time around, her brain was running the show and all that mattered was her child.

Would he agree to the loan? Would he have come in person if he was going to refuse to help her? Surely he would have sent a minion—one of the thousands of people who worked into the night to ensure that the Santoro empire kept multiplying.

'I've already told you that the money isn't for me.' Nervous and self-conscious, she blurted the words out before she could stop herself. 'I don't know what else to do to convince you.'

He turned to face her, his voice soft. 'To be honest, I'm not particularly interested in your reasons for wanting the money. What does interest me is what you intend to give me in return for my—' he lingered over the word thoughtfully '—let's call it an *investment*, shall we?'

There was something in his eyes that made her suddenly wary and nerves flickered in her stomach, her feminine senses suddenly on full alert. 'I don't understand—'

'No?' He moved away from the window. 'Then allow me to give you a basic lesson in business.' His voice was smooth and he watched her with the unflinching gaze of a hunter studying its prey for weakness. 'A business deal is an exchange of favours. No more. No less. I have something you want. You have something I want.'

Feeling as though she was missing something important, her heart beat faster and she licked dry lips with the tip of her tongue. 'I have nothing that you can possibly want. So I assume you're saying no.'

He lifted a hand and trailed a lean, strong finger down her cheek. 'I'm saying that I'm willing to negotiate.' His finger lingered at the corner of her mouth and his smile was disconcerting. 'I will give you money but I want something in return.'

Not his son.

Dear God, please don't let him ask for his son.

Trying to ignore the sudden flip of her stomach, she stared at him helplessly, hardly daring to breathe. 'What?' What else did she have to offer that could possibly be of interest to him? Her flat in London was ridiculously modest by his standards and she had few other assets. 'What is it you want?'

Not Rio. Please, not Rio—

His hand slid into her hair and his eyes didn't shift from hers. 'You.' He said the word with simple clarity. 'I want you, *minha docura*. Back in my bed. Naked. Until I give you permission to get dressed and leave.'

There was a stunned silence. A stunned silence while parts of her body heated to melting point under the raw sexuality she saw in his dark gaze.

She couldn't believe she'd heard him correctly.

He wanted *her?*

Relief that he hadn't mentioned Rio mingled with a shivering, helpless excitement that she didn't understand.

Somehow she managed to speak, but her voice was a disbelieving croak. 'You *can't* be serious.'

'I never joke about sex.'

'But why?' The blood pounded in her ears and she felt alarmingly dizzy. She wished he'd move away from her. *He was too close.* 'Why would you want me in your bed? We've been there, done that—'

His eyes burned into hers. 'And I want to do it again.' He gave a lazy, predatory smile. 'And again. *And again—*'

The air jammed in her lungs. 'You can have any woman you want—'

'Good,' he said silkily, withdrawing his hand from her hair slowly, as if he were reluctant to let her go. 'Then that's settled.'

He stood with his legs planted firmly apart, in full control mode, completely confident that he could manipulate any situation to his advantage.

'Hold on.' She wished desperately that she hadn't taken off the crisp business suit. It was hard to maintain an icy distance dressed in a virtually transparent robe, especially when the conversation was about sex. 'Are you saying that you'll give me the money if I agree to—' she broke off, having difficulty getting her tongue around the words '—sleep with you?'

'Not sleep, no.' His mouth curved into a slow smile that mocked her hesitation. 'I can assure you that there will be very little sleeping involved.'

Her mouth dried and she hugged the robe more closely around herself, as if to protect herself from the feelings that shot through her body. 'It's a ridiculous suggestion.'

Winged dark brows came together in a sharp frown. 'What's ridiculous about it? I'm merely renewing a relationship.'

'A relationship?' Her voice rose. 'We did *not* have a *relationship*, Luc, we had *sex!*' Relentless, mindless, incredible sex that had neutralized her ability to think straight.

Someone in the next room thumped on the wall and Kimberley closed her eyes in embarrassment.

Luc didn't even register the interruption, his handsome face as inscrutable as ever. 'Sex. Relationships.' He shrugged broad shoulders. 'It's all the same thing.'

Her eyes flew wide and she stared at him in appalled dismay. 'No! It is not the same thing, Luc!' She was so outraged she could hardly breathe and she barely remembered to lower her voice. 'It is not the same thing at all! Not that I'd expect a man with your Neanderthal, macho tendencies to understand that.'

He clearly hadn't changed a bit!

Luc shrugged, supremely indifferent to her opinion. 'Women want different things from men, it's an acknowledged fact. I don't need fluffy romantic to make me feel OK about good sex, but if fluffy romantic makes you feel better then that's your choice.'

Her jaw dropped. He just didn't have a clue. 'I can't believe you'd think I'd even *consider* such a proposition. What sort of woman do you think I am?'

'One who needs five million dollars and is willing to do *"absolutely anything"* to get it.' He was brutal in his assessment of the situation. 'I have something you want. You have something I want. This is a business deal at its most basic.'

It was typical of Luc that he viewed sex as just another commodity, she thought helplessly. Typical that he thought he could just buy whatever he wanted. 'What you're suggesting is immoral.'

'It's honest. But you're not that great at being honest about your feelings, are you?' His gaze locked on hers with burning intent. 'Tell me that you haven't lain in your bed at night unable to sleep because you're thinking about me. Tell me that your body doesn't burn for my touch. *Tell me that you're not remembering what it was like between us.*'

Her breathing grew shallow. She didn't want to remember something she'd spent seven years learning to forget.

Kimberley licked dry lips and her stomach dropped. 'You're prepared to pay to go to bed with a woman, Luc?' She struggled to keep her tone light, not to betray just how much he'd unsettled her. 'You must have lost your touch.'

'You think so?' He smiled. 'There is nothing wrong with my touch, *meu amorzinho*, as you will discover the moment you say yes. And, as for paying—' he gave a dismissive shrug '—I can be a very generous lover when I want to be. The money is nothing. Call it a gift. Only this time I will pay you for your services up front to save you the bother of taking the money afterwards.'

Her desperate need for the money warred with her own powerful sense of self-preservation. It had taken her years to recover from the fallout of their relationship. Years to rebuild her life. How could she even contemplate putting herself back in that position?

She knew from bitter experience that he was incapable of connecting with a woman on any level other than the physical. He was incapable of showing or even *feeling* emotion. *He'd break her heart again if she was foolish enough to let him.*

Except that this time she wasn't an idealistic teenager, she reminded herself. Her expectations were realistic. This time round she knew the man she was dealing with. Understood his shortcomings. Understood that he wasn't capable of a relationship.

And, most of all, this time she would have more sense than to fall in love with him.

She almost laughed at her own thoughts. She was weighing up the facts as if she had a decision to make but the truth was there was no decision to make. What choice did she have?

Given the circumstances, how could she say no?

The only thing that mattered was her son.

So what were Luc's reasons? Why would he want her back when he'd been so determined to end their relationship all those years before?

'Why do you want this when our relationship was over years ago?' She just couldn't bring herself to refer to it as sex, even though that was what it had been. 'I just don't understand.'

'Don't you?' His gaze dropped to her mouth and his dark eyes heated with molten sexuality. 'We have unfinished business, *meu amorzinho*, as you well know.'

Her heart thudded hard against her chest. 'I need time to think about it.' *Time to talk herself into doing something that left her almost breathless with panic.*

'You can have ten seconds,' he offered in a smooth tone, glancing around the basic, threadbare room with an expression of appalled distaste. 'And then we're leaving.'

'Ten seconds?' How she wished she'd booked a room with air-conditioning. It was too hot to think properly and she *needed* to think. Just in case there was an alternative—'That's ridiculous! You can't expect me to make a decision that quickly!'

'And yet it was you who said that you needed the money immediately,' he reminded her, thick dark lashes shielding his expression, 'you who told me there was no time to linger over this decision. The blackmailer is waiting, is he not?'

His tone dripped sarcasm and she stared at him helplessly, looking for a hint of softness, a chink in that solid armour plating which might suggest that for him this arrangement was about something deeper than just animal hunger.

But there was nothing soft about Luciano Santoro and no break in the armour. He was hard, ruthless and he took what he wanted.

And it seemed that he wanted her.

'Why?' The words fell from her lips like a plea. 'Why do you want me back? You yourself said that women don't get a second chance with you. It doesn't make sense.'

'It will make perfect sense when you're naked and underneath me,' he assured her in the confident tone of a man who knew a negotiation was all but over. 'Your thinking time is up, *meu amorzinho*. Yes or no?'

She looked at him with loathing, wondering how he could be so cold and detached. Was he capable of feeling *anything*? All her instincts were warning her to say no and run a mile. But then she thought of her son— 'You leave me no choice.'

'How typical of you to pretend that this isn't what you want. Again I'm cast in the role of big bad wolf.' His smile was faintly mocking and he lifted a hand and gently drew his thumb over her lower lip. 'You can always refuse.'

She stared at him, hypnotised by the heat in his eyes.

How? How could she say no, knowing what that would mean for her child?

And yet how could she say yes, knowing what it would mean for her?

'Unfortunately I cannot refuse.' Her voice didn't sound like her own. There was a cold, bitter edge to it that she didn't recognise. 'Unlike you, my commitment to our child is absolute. And to keep him safe I need the money in my account by tonight.'

'My, we are desperate.'

She lifted her chin. 'I'll climb back into your bed, Luc, if that's what it takes, but you'd better be warned. I'm not the same innocent girl you seduced seven years ago. I'm a very different person now. Be sure you know what you're getting. You may not be able to handle me.'

Having agreed to his terms, a tiny part of her refused to let him have it all his own way. Where in their contract did it say that she had to be nice to him?

She didn't feel nice. She didn't feel nice at all.

She was boiling inside and *angry*.

His eyes gleamed dark and his voice lowered to a sexy purr. 'I can handle you with both hands tied behind my back.'

She lifted her chin and her eyes flashed in blatant challenge. 'You can force me into your bed, Luc, but you can't make me enjoy the experience.'

'You think not?'

He moved remarkably quickly for such a powerfully built man, his mouth coming down on hers with a fierce, driving compulsion which shocked and thrilled in equal measure.

It was savage and basic and he stole, plundered and seduced with the warm promise of his mouth and the hot slide of his tongue until her head swirled and her senses exploded.

He kissed with a sexual expertise that made the pleasure roar in her head and she kissed him back, greedy, starved and desperate for more.

And he gave her more. Gave her exactly what he knew she needed.

With a grunt of masculine satisfaction he kissed her deeper, harder, his hands sliding down her back and anchoring her hard against the proud thrust of his arousal. Her starved body melted and hungered for the virile male feel of him and she pressed closer still, her movements feminine and instinctive.

She shivered with wicked excitement and then gave a soft gasp of protest as he dragged his mouth away from hers, leaving her shaking and gasping. She felt the roughness of male stubble graze the soft skin of her cheek and then he released her so suddenly that she almost fell.

'As I said,' he drawled softly, spreading his hands like a magician who had just performed an incredible trick for the benefit of a rapt audience, 'I can handle you with both hands tied behind my back if necessary. No problem.'

Dazed and still fighting the explosion of sensual fireworks that his touch had released, she struggled to bring herself back to the present. Her insides were spinning and her brain was foggy.

If she'd needed proof that she was still vulnerable to Luc Santoro's particular brand of macho sex appeal, then she had it now and she found the knowledge that he could still make her forget everything, just by kissing her, deeply humiliating.

'Thank you for reminding me that I really, *really* hate you.'

'I think I've just proved that you don't.' He gave a shrug that suggested that her feelings were a matter of complete indifference to him. 'And stop pretending that this deal is going to be a hardship to you when we both know you're going to be sobbing and begging the moment I get you back in my bed.'

Goaded past the point of self-control, she lifted a hand and slapped him hard across his lean bronzed cheek—so hard that her palm stung. Shocked and mortified, her hand fell to her side and she stepped back with a gasp of horror.

Never before in her life had she struck anyone or anything, but the image he'd painted of the person she'd been in his bed had been so agonisingly embarrassing that she'd been unable to control herself, and her cheeks flamed at the less than subtle reminder of how eager she'd once been for his caresses. Instantly she vowed that, no matter what happened, *no matter what he did to her,* the next time he touched her she wouldn't respond. She wasn't going to give him the satisfaction. *Whatever it took,* she was going to just lie there.

'You're so wrong about me. I *do* hate you—' Her passionate declaration fell from her lips like a sob. 'I truly hate you for turning me into a person that I don't even recognise.'

'That's because you've conveniently forgotten the person you really are.' He touched long fingers to the livid red streak that had appeared high on his cheek, his expression thoughtful. 'I look forward to reminding you. Over and over again, *meu amorzinho.*'

She stared at him, her chest rising and falling as she struggled to contain the emotion that boiled inside her. 'You're about to discover the woman I really am, Luc, and I just hope it doesn't come as a shock because there's no refund.' She lifted a hand to her throat, struggling to calm herself. 'How long do you expect this charade to last?'

'Until I've finished with you.'

She felt a shaft of maternal panic. 'I have to get home to my son.'

'I don't want to hear any more about this "son",' Luc growled, 'and, just for the record, next time you decide to pin a paternity suit on a guy, don't wait seven years to do it.'

If she'd had a gun she would have shot him for his total insensitivity. Instead she stared at him, angry and frustrated, wondering what she had to do to convince him of Rio's existence. But then she realised that she really didn't *need* him to believe her. All she needed was the money, and it seemed he was willing to give her that.

Providing she agreed to resume their relationship.

She closed her eyes and allowed herself one last frantic attempt to find an alternative, but there wasn't one. And she knew there wasn't one because he had always been her last resort. If there'd been any other conceivable way of raising the money, then she would have found it, but who else could give her five million dollars as easily as blinking?

Her son would be fine without her for a short time, she assured herself firmly, trying to ignore the maternal anxiety that twisted inside her. Jason was like a father to him. Jason would make sure that no harm came to her child. As for her—*she couldn't escape the feeling that she was now in more danger than her child.*

She opened her eyes. 'Two weeks. I can stay no more than two weeks.' She needed to put a time frame on it. Needed to know when she was going home. 'And I didn't pack for a long stay so I'll need to buy something to wear.'

She was proud of her flat, practical tone but he merely smiled in that maddening fashion that never failed to raise her pulse rate. 'Dress by all means, because I have no desire to share your more private attractions with the rest of Brazil, but you don't need to buy anything to wear. For what I have in mind,' he purred softly, 'you're not going to need clothes.'

Her eyes widened. 'But—'

'My car is parked outside and drawing attention even as we speak,' he said smoothly, 'so, unless we wish to begin the second chapter of our relationship the way we began the first, with a brawl on the streets, I suggest we make a move.'

He was no stranger to violence, she knew that from the way he'd handled himself the first night they'd met. And he was no stranger to the darker, rougher side of Rio de Janeiro. But the rumours that he had taken himself from the poverty of the *favelas*, the famed slums of Rio, to billionaire status, had never been confirmed, because Luc Santoro flatly refused to talk about his personal life.

He would talk about the money markets and business in

general, but questions of a more personal nature were skilfully deflected. Luc Santoro remained something of an enigma, which simply served to increase his fascination for the media. *And for women.*

Grabbing her clothes, Kimberley took refuge in the bathroom and dressed quickly. She twisted her hair back on top of her head, buttoned the jacket of her suit and gave her reflection a grim smile. This was a business deal. Nothing more. She was not going to scream or beg. And, most of all, she was *not* going to fall in love.

She almost laughed at the thought.

That was the one aspect of this deal of which she could be entirely confident. There was absolutely *no* risk of her falling in love with him. This time she'd be walking away from the relationship with both her heart and her head in perfect working order.

Drawing confidence from that fact, she opened the bathroom door, picked up her bag and walked towards the door. 'Shall we go?'

Luc cast a disparaging look at the lift and took the stairs. 'If we risk climbing into that thing we may find ourselves stuck for the foreseeable future. Why did you pick this hotel when Rio de Janeiro has so much better to offer?'

Because she'd been saving money.

'It has charm,' she said blithely and his eyes gleamed with appreciative humour.

'If this is the standard that is required to win your approval then I'm not going to have to work very hard to impress you.'

Momentarily transfixed by his smile, her heart gave a tiny flip and then she remembered that Luc used charm like a weapon when it suited him.

'Nothing you do could ever impress me, Luc.'

She'd never been particularly interested in material things.

For her, the true attraction had been the man himself. Luc Santoro approached life with a cool confidence in his own ability to win in every situation. To him, obstacles existed to be smashed down and the greater the problem then the bigger the challenge. And he was a man who loved a challenge. His belief in himself was nothing short of monumental and that, combined with his indecent wealth and staggering dose of sex appeal, made him a prime target for every single woman on the planet.

And he'd chosen her.

There were mornings she'd woken up in his enormous bed, limp and exhausted after a night of relentless sensual exploration, and feasted her eyes on his bronzed male perfection, unable to believe that he was really her man and that this was actually *her life*.

But it hadn't been her life for anywhere near long enough and yet how could anything so perfect ever be anything but ephemeral?

Real life wasn't like that, she reminded herself gloomily as they arrived in the foyer of the hotel. Sixteen years of living with her father had taught her that.

Luc gestured towards the long silver limousine that was parked at the front of the hotel. A driver stood by the open door while a bodyguard stood eyeing the streets around them.

Kimberley frowned. Because Luc was so obviously capable of looking after himself physically, it hadn't really occurred to her that he was a target for crime, but of course he must be, and she gave a little shiver, once more reminded of the letter that lay in her bag.

'Let's go.' His hand was planted firmly in her back but she tried to stop, still reluctant to relinquish her independence.

'I need to settle my bill.'

'You mean they charge to stay in this place?' There was a glimmer of humour in his dark eyes as he urged her into the limousine without allowing her time to pause. 'My staff will deal with it. We need to get out of here before the press arrive, unless you wish to find yourself plastered all over tomorrow's newspapers as an object of speculation for half the world. I have a feeling that *"Woman sold to highest bidder"* would make a very appealing headline for the tabloid press.'

She ignored his sarcasm and frowned slightly. She'd forgotten that Luc Santoro was always an object of press attention and so was any woman seen with him. As one of the richest, most eligible bachelors in the world, it was inevitable that he attracted more than his fair share of media interest and attention.

Out on the street in the sun several flash bulbs went off in her face and Kimberley froze, dazzled and taken by surprise.

'Get into the car,' Luc ordered harshly, just as his bodyguard leaped forward to deal with the photographers.

CHAPTER FOUR

KIMBERLEY slid into the luxurious interior of the vehicle, grateful for the darkened windows that afforded a degree of privacy for those inside.

'How did they know you were here?' She stared at the group of photographers, watching as Luc's bodyguard ushered them out of the way.

'The press follow me everywhere and they also follow anyone who is linked to me in any way,' Luc reminded her in a grim tone, his lean, handsome face taut as he leaned forward and issued a string of instructions to his driver, who promptly accelerated away, leaving the photographers scrambling for their own transport.

'Perhaps if you didn't drive around in a car that shrieks "look at me" you might escape their attention,' she muttered, knowing even as she said the words that it would be virtually impossible for Luc Santoro to be incognito. Everything about him was high profile. He headed up a hugely successful global business and was no stranger to controversy. Added to that, his continued status as a rich playboy meant that he was a constant source of fascination for the world's media. Every woman he was seen with provided days of speculation in the newspapers. *Was this the one? Had a woman finally tamed the Brazilian bad boy?*

It had been the same when she had been with him. They hadn't even been out in public, she recalled bitterly, and yet still the press had managed to snap photos of her climbing into his car. And it had been the media that had alerted her to the fact that he'd left her bed to spend an evening with another woman. *And the media who'd printed pictures of her on the day he'd had her driven to the airport, her expression traumatised, her eyes huge and bruised from too much crying.*

Luc lounged back in his seat, indifferent to what was happening outside the confines of his car. 'I hardly need to remind you that you were the one who chose to book into a hotel in one of the seedier parts of Rio. At least the car is air-conditioned so we can indulge in conversation without risking heatstroke.'

'You were born here. You don't feel the heat.'

He reached across the back of the seat and twisted a coil of her hair around lean bronzed fingers, his eyes trapping hers. 'Whereas you, *minha docura*,' he breathed softly, 'with your blazing hair and your snowy white skin, were designed to be kept indoors in a man's bed, well away from the heat of the sun.'

Her heart thudded against her chest and she felt a vicious stab of sexual awareness deep inside her. 'I prefer the more traditional approach of a hat and sunscreen. And your attitude to women is positively Neolithic.'

The truth was, the heat that could do her the most damage, *the heat that she feared most*, didn't come from the sun.

She felt the gentle pressure on her scalp as he twisted the hair around his fingers and felt her stomach tumble. For a moment she just gazed at him helplessly, captivated by the burning masculine appraisal she saw in his eyes.

It had always begun like this—with his hands in her hair. He'd used her hair as a tool in his seduction. How many times had he murmured that it was the sexiest part of her? How many times had he raked his fingers through the thick copper waves and then wound the strands round his hands to hold her head still for his kiss? Her hair had become an erotic, sensual part of their lovemaking.

Hypnotised by the memories and by the look in his eyes, Kimberley felt a curl of heat low in her pelvis. Her breath jammed in her throat and for a brief, crazy moment her body swayed towards his, lured by the look in his partly veiled eyes and the almost irresistible draw of his hard mouth.

She remembered only too well what that mouth could do to her. *How it felt to be kissed by him.*

And then she also remembered what a cold-hearted, unfeeling man he was and she lifted a hand, removing her hair from his toying fingers with a determined jerk.

'*Don't* touch me—'

'I'm paying you for the privilege of doing just that,' he reminded her in soft tones, 'but I'm prepared to wait until there are no camera lenses around.'

She waited for him to slide back across the seat but he didn't move, his powerful shoulders only inches from hers.

'It's strange that you're so flushed,' he observed in a soft purr, his eyes raking her face. 'Why is that, I wonder?'

She tried to move further away from him but she was trapped against the door of the car with nowhere to go. 'As you yourself pointed out, I'm not great in the heat,' she stammered hoarsely and he gave a knowing smile.

'The car is air-conditioned and we both know perfectly well that it isn't the heat that's bothering you. You want me, *meu amorzinho*, every bit as much as I want you and eventually you're going to stop playing games and admit it.'

Her heart lurched. 'You have an exaggerated opinion of your own attractions,' she said witheringly and he gave a laugh of genuine amusement and slid back across the seat, finally giving her the space she'd thought she craved.

Alarmingly, it didn't seem to make any difference to the growing ache deep in her pelvis. Trapped within the confines of his car, she was still agonizingly aware of his lean, muscular body, sprawled with careless ease in the leather seat.

His phone rang and he gave a frown of irritation as he answered it in his native tongue, switching to rapid, fluent Italian once he identified the caller.

Kimberley watched helplessly, trying not to be impressed by the apparent ease with which he communicated in yet another language, wondering what it was about this man that affected her so deeply. She'd met plenty of handsome men in her time and plenty of clever, successful men. But none of them had once threatened her equilibrium in the way that Luc Santoro did. What was it that made him different? What was it that made her respond to him even though she knew he was so bad for her?

They were *completely* unsuited. They didn't want the same things out of life.

Luc didn't do relationships. Luc just did sex. And the really appalling thing was that he didn't believe there was a difference.

Not for the first time, she wondered what had happened in his life to bring him to that conclusion, but she knew better than to ask. Luc didn't talk about his past. In fact, in the short time they'd spent together, they'd barely talked at all. All their communication had been physical. As a result, she knew next to nothing about him.

He ended the call, snapped the phone shut and she cast a speculative look in his direction.

'Just how many languages do you speak?'

'My business is global, so enough to ensure that everything runs smoothly and I don't get fleeced.' As usual he gave nothing away and she rolled her eyes in exasperation.

'Your conversation skills are so limited that I don't suppose you need a very extensive vocabulary,' she muttered sarcastically. 'You just need to be able to boss people around. You're definitely fluent in He-man.'

He dropped the phone back into his pocket with a laugh. 'It was interesting,' he observed smoothly, 'that you were in my bed for almost a month and only at the end did I see that glorious temper. The signs were always there, of course, only your passion was otherwise directed.'

Kimberley felt a stab of pain as he dropped in yet another reminder of just how uninhibited she'd been during the month they'd spent together. The truth was she'd been so deliriously, ecstatically in love with him that she hadn't seen any reason to hold back. Hadn't realised what sort of man Luc Santoro really was. *Hadn't understood how totally different they were.*

'I hadn't been to bed with a man before,' she said tonelessly. 'It was the novelty factor.' It was a feeble attempt to defend herself and it drew nothing but a mocking gaze from her tormentor.

'The novelty factor?'

Breathing was suddenly a challenge. 'Of course. I was young and I discovered sex for the first time. What did you expect? It would have been the same with anybody.'

'You think so?' His eyes gleamed dark and dangerous as he leaned towards her, his gaze disturbingly intense. 'We barely touched the surface of sensuality,' he drawled huskily, 'but now I think you're ready to be moved on to the next level, *meu amorzinho.*'

Her mouth dried, her heart thudded hard against her chest and suddenly everything around her seemed to be happening in slow motion. She felt a flicker of alarm, mixed with a tinge of an intense excitement that horrified her. 'What do you mean, the next level?'

'Seven years ago you were a virgin. I was your first sexual experience, so naturally I was very careful with you.' His firm mouth curved into a smile of masculine anticipation. 'Now, as you keep reminding me, things are different. The girl is grown up. It's time to discover the woman. This time there will be no holding back.'

Holding back?

Recalling the fierce intensity of their lovemaking, Kimberley wondered exactly what he'd been holding back. She remembered how they'd hungered for each other. She remembered the burning desperation as they slaked their need time and time again. She remembered the heat and the explosive passion. But she didn't remember anything that could have been described as holding back.

Her stomach clenched.

So what exactly did he have in mind this time?

She tore her gaze away from his, horrified by the sexual awareness sizzling through her body. She wanted so badly to feel nothing, to be indifferent, and yet she felt *everything* and the knowledge just appalled her.

She'd spent the last seven years concentrating on making a good life for her child and never once during that time had she experienced even the smallest inclination to become involved with another man.

Her experience with Luc had put her off men completely. It had taken her so long to piece herself back together that she'd assumed she was no longer capable of experiencing such depth of feeling. The discovery that she *was* shocked and horrified her.

It was just physical, she told herself firmly, nothing more than that.

She'd denied herself for so long that it was hardly surprising that her body had reawakened. And so what? She gave a mental shrug. As he rightly said, she was a woman now. She wasn't a naïve girl. She knew that Luc wasn't capable of love and she no longer expected it. They could have sex and then she could walk away back to her old life.

'The question is, can you cope with the woman, Luc?' She threw him a cool, challenging look. 'As you rightly said, the girl has grown up. And, like I said, be careful you don't find yourself with more than you can handle.'

'We've already established that I can handle you.' His dark eyes narrowed. 'And the mere fact that you've agreed to this shows that you are as eager as me to renew our relationship.'

'We didn't have a relationship,' she said flatly. 'We had sex, and I agreed to this because you left me no choice.'

'We always have choices.' For a brief second his expression was bleak and then the moment passed and his eyes held their customary mocking expression. 'It's just that some of them are more difficult than others. That's life.'

She stared at him with mounting frustration. He really thought she was willing to go to bed with him just to satisfy an indecent lust for retail therapy? Did he really have such a low opinion of her?

For a wild moment she was tempted to try one more time to convince him about the existence of his child, but she knew there was no point. 'You're paying me to sleep with you,' she reminded him coldly, 'not to indulge in conversation. That's going to cost you extra.'

Far from being annoyed, he laughed. 'I believe my bank balance will remain unthreatened. You still don't know men very well, *meu amorzinho*. Talking is something that women want, not men. I have no intention of paying you to talk. To be honest, I couldn't care less if you don't speak at all for the next two weeks.'

His gaze shimmered with molten sexuality and suddenly the luxurious interior of the car seemed hotly oppressive. She shifted in her seat, trying desperately to ignore the wicked curl of her stomach.

'Where are we going, anyway?'

He threw her a predatory smile. 'My lair.'

The smooth intimacy of his tone was more than a little disturbing and she felt her breath catch. 'Which one?'

'To my office and from there we'll fly to the island.'

Her fingers curled into her palms. His island. West of Rio was the beautiful Emerald coast, littered with islands, some of them owned by the rich and privileged.

'You mean you're prepared to abandon work?'

'Some things are worthy of my full attention.'

The fact that he was planning to sequester her somewhere secluded increased her tension.

As an impressionable eighteen-year-old, she'd fallen in love with the stunning scenery of this part of Brazil, the forests and the mountains and most of all the beaches. And she'd been overwhelmed by the sheer indulgence of staying on Luc's private island, with all the accompanying luxury and privacy.

During the time they'd spent there, she'd been cocooned in a romantic haze, so sexually sated and madly in love with Luc and the exotic beauty of her surroundings that she couldn't imagine ever wanting to live anywhere else. All her memories of him were tied up with that one special place and she had no desire to return there.

It was just too raw.

'You have other homes,' she croaked. 'Can't we stay somewhere else?'

Somewhere that wouldn't remind her of the past—*of the humiliating completeness of her surrender.* Somewhere that wasn't brimming with memories.

She knew he had an apartment in New York and homes in Paris and Geneva. In fact, one of the reasons she'd chosen to settle in London was because it was the one place where Luc didn't have a home so she was unlikely to bump into him.

His eyes gleamed with masculine amusement. 'For what I have in mind, I require privacy and the island is perfect for that. And anyway—' he gave a careless shrug '—I'm still close enough to the office to be able to fly back if necessary.'

'Business. Business. Business.' She stared at him in exasperation, her nerves jumping and her senses humming. 'Is that all you ever think of?'

'No.' His reply was a sensual purr. 'I also think about sex. Like now, for instance.' He leaned his head back against the seat, his expression inscrutable. 'I'm cursing the need for me to return to the office to sign some papers when all I want to do is fly straight to the island and strip you naked.'

His words should have shocked her, but instead a wicked thrill flashed through her and her tummy muscles tightened. Suddenly she was aware of every masculine inch of him and just hated herself for feeling excitement when what she wanted to feel was indifference. 'You have a totally one track mind, do you know that?'

She told herself that it didn't matter what she felt as long as she didn't reveal those feelings to him. Last time she'd offered every single part of herself and he'd rejected her. This time she would give nothing except her body.

'If by "one track mind" you mean that I know what I want and I make sure that I get it, then yes—' he gave a lethal smile '—I have a one track mind. And as soon as these papers are signed, my mind is going to be on you, *meu amorzinho,* and you're going to discover just how fixed on one track my mind can be.'

His gaze slid down her body in a leisurely scrutiny and she struggled and fought against the wicked excitement that burned low in her pelvis.

He was the sexiest man she'd ever encountered, Kimberley thought helplessly, dragging her eyes away from his shimmering dark eyes and staring out of the car window in quiet desperation. She didn't want to notice anything about him, but instead she found herself noticing *everything*.

Determined not to sink under his seductive spell a second time, she tried to talk some sense into herself.

Sexy wasn't enough.

She reminded herself that this man was a control freak who was incapable of feeling or expressing normal human emotions.

She reminded herself that he'd taken her heart and chopped it into a million tiny pieces.

She reminded herself that she'd spent years building a new life after their scorching, intense, but all too brief relationship had ended.

Suddenly aware that the car had stopped, she realised that she'd barely even noticed the journey. All her attention had been focused on Luc.

A perfectly normal reaction, she tried to assure herself as she unfastened her seat belt. She hadn't seen him for years and he was the father of her child. They shared plenty of history. It was understandable that she'd find him impossible to ignore.

His driver held the door for her and she stepped out. For a wild moment she was tempted to turn and run along the sunbaked pavement and lose herself in the streets of Rio, but her bag was on her shoulder and in her bag was the letter.

The letter that had changed her life.

She wasn't in a position to run anywhere.

She needed five million dollars and the only man who could give her that was Luc Santoro.

And perhaps he read her mind because he paused for a moment on the pavement, watching her with those amazingly sexy dark eyes. Then he placed a hand firmly in the small of her back and walked her into the building.

'Loitering on pavements is not an occupation to be commended,' he observed dryly, striding towards the express lift without looking left or right, very much the king of his domain.

He urged her inside, hit a button and the doors slid together, closing out the outside world. A tense, intimate silence folded around them. Suddenly she was breathlessly, helplessly aware that she was alone in this confined space with the one man capable of turning her perfectly ordered life upside down.

Struggling to control the tiny tremors that shook her body, Kimberley stared at the floor but she felt the attraction pulsing between them like the pull of a magnet.

With a quiet desperation she risked a glance at him, expecting to find him watching the passage of the lift upwards. Instead their eyes locked and the last of her sanity fizzled out, torched by the sexual awareness that flared between them.

His handsome features grim and set, he gave a harsh curse and powered her back against the wall of the lift, his mouth hard and hungry as he kissed her with unrelenting passion.

Driven to fever pitch by the tension that had been mounting between them since she'd walked back into his office less than twenty-four hours earlier, she kissed him back, their tongues blending, her desperation more than matching his.

Her arms slid round his neck and her fingers jammed into his dark hair as he took her mouth with erotic expertise, exploring and seducing until her body was humming with unrelieved sexual need and her mind was numb. Every rational thought slid from her brain and she ceased to be a thinking, intelligent woman. Instead she responded with almost animal desperation, her head swimming with a wild hunger that was outside her control.

His eyes still burning into hers, he released a throaty groan of masculine appreciation and, without lifting his mouth, he yanked her skirt upwards and his hands slid down to her bottom. He hauled her hard against him and she gave a gasp of shock as she felt the unmistakable thrust of his erection against her.

The last of her resistance fell away to be replaced by a driving need so basic and powerful that she was completely controlled by its force. Her body throbbed and ached and cried out for satisfaction while her heart raced madly in a flight of excitement.

She forgot all her resolutions. Forgot all the promises she'd made to herself.

Instead she yanked at his shirt and slid her hands underneath, needing to touch, *to feel*, just desperate to get closer to him. Her seeking fingers found warm flesh, male body hair and hard muscle and she moaned her pleasure against his mouth as her starved senses leapt into overdrive and her body awakened.

She'd denied herself for so long that there was no hope of denying herself now. Not when what she needed so badly was standing right in front of her.

She felt every male inch of him pumped up and hard against her, and then his hands tore aside her panties and he lifted her, crashing her back against the wall with a thud as he took the weight of her body, his fingers digging hard into her thighs.

The lift gave a muted 'ping' but he merely reached out and thumped a button with an impatient hand, his eyes never leaving her eyes, his mouth never lifting from her mouth.

Helpless with excitement, Kimberley curled her legs around him, driven by an urgency that she didn't understand, her body throbbing with almost agonising excitement.

'Luc, please—' She sobbed his name into his mouth and moved her hips in a desperate plea for satisfaction and he gave a low grunt and cupped her with his hand.

Immediately Kimberley exploded into a climax so intense that she could hardly breathe. And still he kissed her, trapping her wild cries and sobs with his mouth as he slid his fingers deep inside her, his touch so shockingly intimate and amazingly skilled that the agonizing spasms just went on and on. She trembled and gasped, trapped on a sexual plateau until finally her body subsided.

Only then did he lift his mouth from hers, his breathing harsh and ragged as he scanned her flushed cheeks.

Gradually her own breathing slowed and her vision cleared and she became aware of exactly what she'd just done. *What she'd let him do to her.* In a public place.

'*Meu Deus*—' As if realising the same thing, he lowered her to the floor, streaks of colour highlighting his stunning bone structure as he lowered her to the floor. 'I don't know myself when I'm with you.'

His breathing was far from steady and his dark hair was roughened where her fingers had tugged and pulled. Still without uttering a word, he gently freed himself from the twisting, clinging coils of her fiery hair.

Tangled and wild from his hands and her own frantic movements, it tumbled in total disarray over her shoulders, half obscuring her vision.

Which was just as well, she reflected miserably as she ducked her head and tried frantically to straighten her clothing, because she couldn't bring herself to look at him and her hair provided a convenient curtain.

Deeply shocked by her own behaviour, she wanted to slink into a dark hole and never re-emerge.

She'd done it again.

For the past seven years she'd had absolutely no trouble resisting men. And it hadn't been for a lack of invitations. In fact she'd been so uninterested in the opposite sex that she'd assumed that her relationship with Luc had killed something inside her. And she'd been hugely relieved by that knowledge. It meant that her one all-consuming experience of love had rendered her immune to another attack of a similar nature. It meant that she was never again at risk of experiencing that out of control burning desire for a man, which had left her broken-hearted and soaked with humiliation.

How wrong could she have been?

Five seconds in an enclosed space with Luc was all it had taken for her to revert to her old self. She responded to him in the most basic animal fashion and no amount of logic or reason seemed to quell the burning need she had for him. The searing attraction between them was more powerful than common sense and lessons learned. So powerful that it outweighed all other considerations.

Like the fact that they were in a public lift.

Suddenly aware of their surroundings and the risk they'd just taken, various scenarios flashed across her brain and she lifted her head and stared at him in horror. 'Someone could have called the lift—'

For a long pulsing moment he didn't speak and she had a vague feeling that he was as stunned as she was, but then he stepped away from her and gave a casual shrug.

'Then they would have had a shock,' he drawled, adjusting his own clothing with a characteristic lack of concern for the opinion of others.

'You may be into public displays, but I'm not.'

In response he stroked a leisurely finger down her burning cheek. 'As usual you appear to be blaming me, but face it, *meu amorzinho*, you were as hot for it as I was. You didn't know where you were or what you were doing.' As if to prove his point, he stooped to retrieve something from the floor. 'These are yours, I believe.'

Kimberley stared down at the torn panties he'd given her and wanted to sink to the bottom of the lift shaft. Before she had a chance to comment, he stretched out a hand, hit a button on a panel on the wall and the lift doors opened.

Furious with him for not giving her more time to compose herself and still shrinking with mortification,

Kimberley was forced to stuff the remains of her underwear into her handbag. She stared after him with growing frustration and anger as he strolled out into his suite of offices without a backward glance in her direction, and for a wild moment she was tempted to take the lift back down to the ground floor and make a run for it. How could he seem so indifferent? He was totally relaxed and in control, as if indulging in mind-blowing sex in a lift was an everyday occurrence for him.

And perhaps it was, she reflected miserably as she reminded herself of the reason she was here and forced herself to follow him, her heels tapping on the polished marble floor. Women threw themselves at Luc Santoro wherever he went. She was sure there were endless numbers of females only too eager to indulge in a spot of elevator-sex with a drop dead gorgeous billionaire, given the opportunity.

Spotting a door marked 'Ladies', Kimberley took the opportunity to slip inside and do what she could to rectify her appearance.

When she emerged she saw that Luc was talking to the same personal assistant who had brought her the water and shown her such kindness.

She possessed the same exotic dark looks as her boss, but she was about twenty years older than Kimberley would have expected. Somehow she'd assumed that his personal assistant would be young and provocative.

The woman ended a phone call and gave her boss a wry smile. 'Well, you've stirred them all up as usual.'

'Is everything arranged?'

'You just need to check these figures, sign these because the fifth floor lot almost passed out with horror when I told them that you were planning to be out of the office—' she pushed some papers in his direction '—and everything else I can cope with. I'll speak to Milan about rescheduling that

presentation and Phil will be over from New York next
Wednesday as you requested. All sorted.'

'The helicopter?'

'Your pilot is waiting for you both.'

Horribly self-conscious and uncomfortably sure that, despite her attempts to freshen up her make-up, the evidence of
their passionate encounter must be somehow visible,
Kimberley hovered in the background, wondering how Luc
could make the shift from hot lover to cool-headed businessman with such casual ease.

There was no trace of the hungry, passionate, out of control man who'd driven her to vertiginous heights of sexual
pleasure only moments earlier.

Instead he seemed icy cold and more than a little remote
and detached, his mind well and truly back on business as he
scanned the papers and held his hand out for a pen.

Sex and business—the only two things that interested him
in life.

Clearly their steamy encounter in the lift hadn't affected
him in the same way it had affected her, Kimberley thought,
and the knowledge depressed her more than she cared to
admit. Even in the bedroom their relationship was one-sided.
He turned her into a shivering, sobbing wreck, willing to do
anything for his touch, while he was perfectly capable of
walking away from their steamy encounters with equa-
nimity.

*She had a horrid lowering feeling that she could have
been anyone.*

Glancing at his lean, handsome profile, she decided that
there was nothing to suggest that he'd shared anything but polite conversation with the woman who had been his compan-
ion in the lift. In total contrast, her own body was still
throbbing from the intimacies they'd shared. Her heart was
pounding and her lips were sore and swollen from his touch

and she was sure that it must be completely obvious to anyone who cared to look at her that their trip in the lift hadn't involved a single moment of conversation.

Having handed Luc another file, the older woman looked across and gave her a slightly harassed apologetic smile. *'Como vai você?* How are you? I'm Maria. Sorry to hold you up but we weren't expecting him to be out of the office next week. He just needs to take a look at these figures for me, then you can go off and spoil yourselves.'

Spoil themselves?

Kimberley looked at her in consternation, not sure how to respond. Just how much did his PA know about their deal? She made it sound as though they were going to take a holiday. And Luc's proposed absence was clearly causing no end of problems for everyone. She glanced back at him but he had his eyes on the screen, scanning the figures.

He made a few comments, signed the rest of the papers and then glanced at his watch in an impatient gesture. Restless energy pulsed from his powerful frame and he closed lean, strong fingers around her wrist and hauled her against his side in a proprietary gesture.

'Enough. Let's go.' Like a man on a mission, he virtually dragged her across the floor and through the glass doors that led directly to the roof of the building and the helicopter pad.

His pilot and another man who Kimberley assumed to be another bodyguard immediately snapped to attention as Luc strode towards them, a look of purposeful intent in his shimmering dark gaze.

'There's no need to drag me,' she muttered, stumbling to keep up with him and he flashed her a smile that was nothing short of predatory.

'I'm in a hurry. It's either this or we go straight back in that lift. Take your pick.'

She shot him a look of naked exasperation. 'Your behaviour is well and truly locked in the Stone Age, do you know that? Have you ever even heard of the feminist movement and equal opportunities?'

'You will certainly have equal opportunity to experience pleasure once you're in my bed,' he assured her in silky tones, nodding to the pilot as he urged her into the helicopter with an almost indecent degree of haste.

Left with no choice, she slid into the nearest seat and shot him a look of helpless disbelief. 'You're unbelievable. Do any women actually agree to work for you?'

'Of course.' He loosened his tie and gave a tiny frown, clearly thinking it an odd question. 'You just met Maria.'

'Yes, she wasn't at all what I expected.' Kimberley's fingers tightened on her bag. She was horribly conscious of his proximity and the quivering, aching response of her own body, which seemed to be totally outside her control. No matter what she thought or what she wanted, it seemed she was destined to be fatally drawn to his raw male sex appeal.

Dangerous black eyes gleamed with amusement as he fastened his seat belt. 'And just what were you expecting?'

Kimberley looked away from him and focused on a point outside the window. 'I don't know. Someone younger? More glamorous. You're addicted to beautiful women.' *As she'd discovered to her cost.* For a short blissful time, she'd thought he was addicted to *her* and then she'd discovered just how short his attention span was. He'd cured his addiction to her all too easily.

'The secret of success in business is to be clear about the job description and then select the right person for the job,' he informed her in cool tones. 'The attributes I require in a PA are not the same as those I require in my bedroom. I never confuse the two roles and I never mix business with pleasure.'

This evidence of his ruthless self-discipline was in such stark contrast to her own dismal lack of control when she was around him that she felt her frustration slowly mounting. Was he really able to be that detached?

Recalling the way he'd strolled out of the lift and clicked his mind into business mode, she decided that he clearly was and the realisation wasn't flattering.

Evidently the effect she had on him was less than overwhelming.

She glanced across at him. 'So what would you do if you wanted a relationship with someone who worked for you?'

'Fire them and then sleep with them,' he replied without hesitation. 'But I don't understand why that would interest you. You're not working for me, so there's absolutely no barrier to our relationship.'

'Apart from the fact that we can't stand the sight of one another.'

'Cast your mind back to the lift,' he suggested silkily, dark lashes lowering as he studied her with blatantly sexual intent. 'And if that doesn't jog your memory, then try asking yourself why you're not currently wearing underwear.'

She gave a tiny gasp of shock and her heart skipped a beat. 'You didn't give me the opportunity to put them back on, they were in tatters,' she murmured, trying without any confidence of success to emulate the cool indifference that he constantly displayed.

'That's because I believe in economy of effort and I don't see the point in removing them twice.'

'Aren't you ever interested in anything other than sex?' she blurted out suddenly. 'Don't you want to know a single thing about me?'

'I know that you excite me more than any woman I've ever met,' he responded instantly, night-black eyes raking her tense, quivering body with raw masculine appreciation. 'What else would I want, or need, to know?'

She gazed at him helplessly, both fascinated and appalled by his total lack of emotional engagement. He was a man who operated alone. A man who appeared to need no one.

Luc didn't have a single vulnerable bone in his body.

Then she thought of Rio and she was stifled by a maternal love so powerful that it almost choked her.

In a sudden rush of panic, she fumbled for her seat belt and unclipped it. 'I can't do this, Luc, I'm sorry,' she stammered. 'You have to take me to the airport. I have to go home now. I need to be there for my son. I've never left him before, not for this long, and he's in danger—'

Luc lounged in his seat, watching her with interest. 'Drop the act, *meu amorzinho*,' he advised gently. 'The money is already paid. The deal is done.'

Her breathing quickened. 'But what if it isn't enough?' She bit her lip. 'Don't blackmailers often come back for more?'

Luc paused, his eyes glittering dark in his handsome face. 'I think it will take our "blackmailer" a little while to work her way through five million dollars, don't you?' His tone was mocking and she flushed with anger and frustration.

'You're making *such* a big mistake.'

'I don't make mistakes. I make decisions and they're always the right ones,' he said in a cool tone, 'and my decision on this is to pay you what you've asked for. It's done. Now you have to play your part and I don't want to hear any more mention of blackmailers or sweet, vulnerable children who need you at home.'

What could she do?

The helicopter was already in mid-flight and, if what Luc said was correct, then the money was already in the hands of the blackmailer.

Kimberley turned her head so that he couldn't see the tears in her eyes.

This was about *her*, not her son, she acknowledged helplessly. She'd always been hideously over-protective. From the moment Rio was born, her love for him had been absolute and unconditional. She'd tried hard not to smother him but she found it incredibly hard. She just loved him *so* much and she couldn't bear the thought that anything might make him unhappy, even for a moment.

But Rio would be fine, she told herself firmly. He adored Jason and Jason adored him back and would never let anything happen to him.

It was she who was going to suffer by not being close to her child.

Two weeks. She straightened her narrow shoulders and forced herself to get a grip on her emotions. Just two weeks and then her life would be back to normal again.

No blackmailer and no Luc.

Would it really be that hard? What was he asking for? Sex without love?

Well, she could do that.

She was just going to lie there, she vowed fiercely to herself. She wasn't going to sob and she wasn't going to beg.

And when eventually she bored him and he decided to let her go, she was going to walk away without a backward glance, as emotionally detached as he was.

CHAPTER FIVE

THE helicopter had barely settled on dry land before Luc was out of his seat. If he was aware of the mystified glances exchanged between his bodyguards and his pilot then he gave no sign, his darkly handsome face a mask of cool indifference as he strode the short distance to the villa with Kimberley clamped firmly by his side.

For a man who prided himself on his rigid self-discipline and self-control, he was suffering from no small degree of discomfort and irritation because at that precise moment he'd never felt *less* in control. Only once before in his life could he remember acting in such a wild and impulsive manner and that was seven years before when Kimberley had first entered his life.

The knowledge did nothing to soothe his volatile and uncertain mood.

He was frustrated, exasperated and more than a little disturbed by his own behaviour, and he didn't need to read the body language of his clearly stunned staff to confirm that his behaviour was totally out of character.

It wasn't just the incident in the lift, he mused grimly as he walked with single-minded purpose through the grounds of the villa, indifferent to the visual temptation presented by the lush gardens. His fingers were still clamped around her slender wrist as he headed directly for the master suite, skirting round the tempting blue of the pool, which sparkled and shimmered in the sunlight.

No. It definitely wasn't about the lift. What did that prove, apart from the fact that he was a normal red-blooded guy with a healthy appetite for an attractive woman and an ability to make the most of the moment?

He could even have dismissed the more seedy aspects of seducing a woman in a public place if the experience had left him clear-headed and sated and with his sanity fully restored. But that wasn't the case. Like an alcoholic who had allowed himself the dark indulgence of just one drink, that one taste of the forbidden had left him with a throbbing, nagging need for still more and he had an uncomfortable feeling that even a gawking crowd wouldn't be enough to tempt him to exercise restraint should the situation arise again.

And that was what he found uncomfortable about the whole situation in which he now found himself.

He never lost control. In fact he prided himself on his ability to remain cool when others around him were reaching boiling point. He prided himself on his ability to maintain a rational approach to decision making when others around him became emotional. It was his ability to think, unencumbered by the emotional baggage that seemed to trouble some people, which was a major contributor to his current success.

And, although women played an important part in his life, never *ever* had a woman compromised his business decisions.

Until now.

From the moment Kimberley had re-entered his life, all that mattered to him was getting her back in his bed and keeping her there until his body was sufficiently sated for him to be able to think clearly again.

His behaviour since Kimberley had walked back into his

life had been so completely out of character that he was not in the least surprised that his bodyguards and pilot were looking at him strangely. Even Maria, who knew more about him than most, had been openly shocked by his sudden request that she completely rearrange his diary in order to accommodate his need to be absent from the office for the foreseeable future. In fact he was entirely sure that a large proportion of his staff would be huddled together at this very moment discussing the question of their boss's personality transformation.

And he was asking himself the very same question.

Given the delicate stage of the business deal he was currently negotiating, it was nothing short of reckless to cancel meetings and leave the office at a time when his presence was mandatory.

But that was exactly what he'd done and he was ready to ignore the consequences.

He was ready to ignore everything except the building sexual tension that nagged at his body. Their torrid encounter in the lift had succeeded in heating his blood to intolerable levels and, if it hadn't been for the fact that halting the lift for any longer would have attracted the attentions of a maintenance team with embarrassing consequences, he would have satisfied his baser urges and taken her there and then, against the mirrored wall of his express lift.

The knowledge would have disturbed him more had he not been grimly aware that there had never been a woman who had succeeded in holding his attention longer than a few weeks. Given that knowledge, he was entirely confident that, with the right degree of dedication to the task in hand, he could easily work Kimberley out of his system.

She really was pushing her luck, he mused, trying to slap him with a paternity suit seven years after their relationship had ended. Did she think he was entirely stupid? Still, her greed had thrown her back into his path and for that he was grateful. He'd been given the chance to get her out of his system once and for all.

This time he was going to take the relationship to its inevitable conclusion.

Despite the number of corporate headaches bearing down on him from all sides, he'd decided to dedicate the next few weeks of his life to becoming bored by Kimberley. He owed it to his sanity and his ability to concentrate. And all he required to fulfil that task was privacy and an extremely large double bed, both of which were very much available in his villa. It was the one place in the world where he was guaranteed not to be disturbed. The one place where the press and the public were unable to gain any sort of access.

The one place where he could be truly alone to concentrate on Kimberley.

And, if the episode in the lift was anything to go by, they really, *really* needed to be alone.

Hot, sticky and thoroughly overheated by factors far more complex than a tropical climate, Kimberley glanced longingly at the cool water of the pool, but Luc didn't alter his pace as he strode towards the bedroom suite that she remembered all too well.

Her pulse rate increased and her mouth dried.

During the time they'd spent on the island she'd hardly left that room and going back there now simply intensified the shame she already felt at the uninhibited way she'd responded to him all those years ago.

She wanted to dig her heels in and resist but the tight grip of his strong fingers on her wrist and the grim, set expression on his face were warning enough that any argument on her part was futile.

And anyway, she reasoned helplessly, how could she argue?

She'd agreed to this.

For the sum of five million dollars and to protect her child, she'd agreed to it and she just wanted to get the next two weeks over with as quickly as possible and get home.

She wanted to be with her son. She missed him dreadfully.

And she was afraid. Desperately afraid that she might turn back into the helpless, needy woman Luc had seduced all those years before.

When she'd met him she'd been a hard working, successful model. She'd never missed a shoot or been late for an appointment in her life. Then she'd met Luc and all that had changed.

One hot glance from those dark eyes and she'd been dazzled, unable to see anything except *him.* She'd abandoned her job, forgotten her responsibilities and ceased to care about anything except Luc.

She'd been so drunk on her love for him that she'd failed to see that, for him, their relationship was all about sex. Even when he'd left her in bed to date other women, she hadn't truly accepted that their relationship had no future. Only when she'd discovered that she was pregnant, only when she'd turned to him for help and been rejected, had she finally accepted that it was over.

And now here she was, about to walk back into Luc Santoro's bedroom again. *About to risk everything.*

Last time he'd hurt her so badly with his cruel indifference that it had taken years for her to piece her life back together again, but she'd done it and she was proud of the woman she'd become. Proud of her son and the small business she'd built. Proud of her life. And she'd been very careful to preserve and protect that life.

But this wasn't like the last time, she reminded herself firmly. The last time she'd been young, naïve and hopelessly in love with the man she'd wanted Luc to be. Now she was a very different person and, no matter how powerful the sexual attraction, she wasn't going to lose sight of the man he really was. She had no intention of making that mistake a second time in her life.

She knew now that Luc didn't have an emotional bone in his perfectly put together body and he was never going to change.

She lifted her chin. He'd proved to her time and time again that he was capable of enjoying sex without emotion, so why shouldn't she be able to do the same thing? In many ways he was the perfect man for the task, she thought, sneaking a sideways glance at his hard, handsome profile. Whatever criticisms could be levelled at him in the emotional stakes, his bedroom technique was surely unsurpassed.

Remembering the wild, mindless encounter in the lift, her breathing hitched in her throat and a sudden flare of delicious, forbidden excitement scorched her body.

She would approach the next two weeks with the same emotional detachment that he did, she vowed silently, ignoring the bump of her heart as he all but dragged her into the bedroom that opened directly on to the pool area.

In front of her was a huge bed, *the* huge bed that she remembered well. She should do, she thought wryly, because she had barely left it for the entire time they'd spent at the villa.

Covered with sheets of the finest Egyptian cotton, it faced both the pool and the sea, but Kimberley recalled with a lowering degree of clarity that on the previous occasion she'd lain in that very bed and been totally unaware of the view. When she had been with Luc, for her the outside world had ceased to exist.

Well, not any more.

This time she was going to enjoy the pool and the sea along with any other hidden delights that his private island had to offer.

She'd enjoy the sex for the two weeks, just as she'd agreed, but this time everything else would be different. She'd enjoy his incredible body in the most superficial way possible. She wasn't going to fall in love and she wasn't going to pretend that Luc might fall in love with *her*.

That way she'd be sure of being able to walk away with her heart completely intact.

If he could do it, so could she, and just to prove that fact she turned to him with a cool smile on her face.

'Well—' She waved a hand towards the bed in an almost dismissive gesture. 'We seem to have everything we need, so shall we make a start?'

Wasn't that what it was all about? Practicality versus romance.

She just needed to learn to play by different rules. *His rules*.

His dark eyes sharpened on her face. 'Sarcasm doesn't suit you. It isn't part of your personality and it isn't part of who you are.'

'You have no idea who I am, Luc, and we both know that it isn't my personality that interests you.' She kept her tone casual as she strolled towards the bed and dropped her bag on the cover. 'And you're the one who keeps reminding me that you didn't pay five million dollars to indulge in conversation.'

She saw the flicker of incredulity cross his handsome face and suddenly felt like smiling.

He'd expected her to stammer and protest. He'd been prepared to control and dominate in his usual fashion. But this time she wasn't going to allow it. This time, she was the one with the upper hand. Instead of fighting against the tide she was swimming with it.

She'd surprised him and it felt *good*.

With a sense of power and confidence that she couldn't ever remember feeling before in his company, she casually undid the buttons of her shirt and strolled towards the luxurious bathroom. 'I'll just take a shower and I'll meet you in the bed in five minutes.'

She was doing brilliantly, she told herself gleefully as she stripped her clothes off and stepped under the power shower. Even though this situation wasn't of her choice, there was no reason why she had to allow Luc to call all the shots.

The spray was the perfect temperature and she closed her eyes and gave a soft moan of pleasure as the cool water drenched her heated flesh.

For a moment she just stood there, humming softly to herself, revelling in the feel of the water on her skin and the knowledge that, for once, she was the one in control.

Her feeling of smug satisfaction lasted all of eight seconds.

'I never knew you had such a good singing voice,' came a dark male drawl from directly next to her and with a soft gasp of shock she opened her eyes and brushed the water away from her face to clear her vision.

Luc stood only inches away from her, gloriously naked and unashamedly aroused, his body as close to male physical perfection as it was possible to get.

'I must congratulate you.' The water clung to his thick, dark lashes and he watched her with a slumberous expression in his wicked dark eyes. 'A shower together was the perfect idea, *meu amorzinho*. I more than approve.'

Her new-found confidence vanished in an instant.

He wasn't supposed to approve. He was supposed to be feeling deflated and frustrated and slightly at a loss by the fact she'd taken control.

Instead he looked like a man who was well and truly in command of the situation.

Remembering her promise to herself not to play the part of the shrinking maiden, she resisted the temptation to flatten herself against the wall of the shower.

'You didn't need to join me,' she said in a cool voice, averting her eyes from the tantalising vision of curling black hair shadowing a bronzed, muscular chest. She didn't dare look lower. Her one brief glimpse when she'd opened her eyes had been more than enough to remind her of his undeniable masculinity. 'We have a contract and I intend to honour it. You don't need to worry about me escaping.'

'Do I look worried?' His eyes gleamed dark with amusement and he lifted a hand and smoothed her damp hair away from her face. 'Why would I worry when I know you can't say no to me?'

She gritted her teeth and tried to ignore the tiny spasms of excitement that licked through her body. 'You need a private island to accommodate your ego.'

He gave a soft laugh and reached out to pull her closer in a gesture that was pure caveman. 'I love the fact that you pretend you can resist me. It's going to make your final surrender all the more satisfying. You present me with a challenge and I *love* a challenge.'

She stared at him helplessly, appalled by his arrogance and yet fascinated by his undiluted masculinity. 'What you're saying is that you just can't take no for an answer.'

'Perhaps my English isn't always perfect.'

'Your English is f-fluent,' she stammered, heat piercing through her pelvis as the roughness of his thighs brushed against her bare legs. 'It's just that you always have to get your own way in everything.'

'And what's wrong with that?' He gave a casual shrug and curved an arm around her narrow waist, bringing her hard against him. 'Especially when we both want the same thing.'

Her heart was thumping so hard that she could hardly breathe and as she felt him reach for the soap and slide his hands down her bare back she couldn't hold back the moan.

'You have an amazing body,' he said hoarsely, turning her round and sliding his strong hands down her spine.

Her eyes closed and she forced herself to think about something else. But the only thing in her mind was Luc and when she felt his hands move to her hair she gave a shudder of approbation.

He lathered her hair, his fingers delivering a slow, sensual massage to her scalp, and she closed her eyes, unable to resist the amazingly skilful pressure of his fingers. It had always been like this, she thought helplessly as she sank into his caress. He knew exactly how to touch her. Exactly how to melt resistance. *Exactly how to drive her wild.*

He washed the rest of her body, lingering in some parts just long enough to make her squirm and then moving on to concentrate his attentions elsewhere.

He carried on until her entire body was quivering with anticipation. *Until she was desperate to explore him the way he was exploring her.* Unable to wait a moment longer, Kimberley reached out and slid a hand over his chest and then lower still, following the track of dark hair that led downwards.

But he caught her wrists in his hands and drew her arms round his neck, refusing her the satisfaction of touching him.

Need and frustration pounding in her veins, she tried to free her arms but he held her firm, a glimmer of mockery in his dark eyes as he lowered his mouth to hers.

But he refused to kiss her properly.

Still in teasing mode, he licked at the corners of her mouth, played with her lower lip and kissed his way down her neck until she was gasping and writhing against him, but still he wouldn't give her what she craved.

Her whole body throbbed and ached with an intensity that approached pain, but there was nothing she could do to relieve the mounting frustration. Only he could do that and he was careful to give her just enough to build the excitement while withholding the ultimate satisfaction that she craved.

He teased her and seduced her until every nerve in her body was throbbing and humming, until she was unable to think about anything except the man in front of her. Her mind ceased to function and she was driven entirely by her senses to the point where she wasn't even aware that he'd switched off the shower until she felt herself wrapped in a soft towel and lifted into his arms.

Somewhere in the back of her mind something nagged at her. Something about him being the one in control once more. But she couldn't hold on to the thought long enough to examine it, let alone act on it, so she lay still in his arms, drugged and dizzy from his slow, expert seduction.

He laid her on the bed, removed the towel with a gentle but determined tug and then came down on top of her, a gleam of masculine purpose in his dark eyes.

Almost breathless with desperation, she ran her hands down the sleek muscle of his back and shifted her body under his in an attempt to gain access to the male power of him. He slid away from her in a smooth movement and she gave a sob of frustration, her hips writhing against the sheets.

'You touch me—why can't I touch you?'

'Not yet—' He anchored her wrists in his hands and held them above her head and then finally he lowered his head to hers.

His mouth took hers in a kiss so hot and sexual that the room spun around her and she thought she might actually lose consciousness.

His tongue explored every inch of her mouth with erotic expertise and she was so drugged by his skilful touch that she didn't realise that he'd tied her wrists until she tried to slide her arms round his neck and discovered that she couldn't.

Her hands were firmly secured to the head of the bed.

He gave a low laugh of masculine satisfaction and slid down her body. 'Now I have you *exactly* where I want you, *meu amorzinho.*'

A flicker of alarm penetrated the sensual fog that had paralysed her brain and she tried to tug at her wrists but he chose that precise moment to flick his tongue over her nipple and she gave a gasp as sharp needles of sensation pierced her body.

She writhed and shifted on the bed, trying desperately to rediscover her powers of speech and demand that he let her go, when he sucked her into his mouth and proceeded to subject her to the skill of his tongue.

It was maddeningly good and she felt the burning ache in her pelvis increase to almost intolerable levels but he was in no hurry, his seduction slow and leisurely as he skilfully caressed first one breast and then the other.

She squirmed and gasped and tugged at her bound wrists and just when she thought she couldn't stand it any longer he slid down her body.

Barely able to form the words, she gave a moan of protest, horribly embarrassed. 'Untie me, Luc, please—'

He lifted his dark head, 'Not yet. You still have too many inhibitions. You think too much. I want to show you what your body can feel when the freedom of choice is removed. You are quite safe, *meu amorzinho*. All that is going to happen is that I intend to torture you with pleasure and you will be totally unable to resist.'

Horror and disbelief mingled with a sense of wicked anticipation as he slid further down the bed and closed his strong hands round her trembling thighs.

Realising his intention, she tried desperately to keep her legs together, but he gave a low laugh and ignored her feeble resistance, opening her to his hungry gaze with the gentle pressure of his hands.

She'd never felt so exposed before, so vulnerable, and her face burned hot under his probing, masculine gaze. Her whole body tensed as she felt his fingers slide through the fiery curls at the apex of her thighs and then he was parting her and she felt the damp flick of his tongue exploring her intimately.

She gave a gasp of shock and tried to free herself but her hands were securely tied and she had no way of protecting herself from his determined seduction. And soon the very thought of protecting herself vanished from her brain because what he was doing to her body felt so impossibly, exquisitely good she thought there was a very strong chance that she might pass out.

When he slid his fingers deep inside her, Kimberley shot into a climax so intense that she cried out sharply in almost agonised disbelief. The sensation went on and on, his fingers and his mouth witness to the sensual havoc he was creating within her body.

It was so wild that she lost touch with reality, lost touch with everything, controlled entirely by erotic sensation caused by one man.

Finally the spasms eased and he slid up her body in a smooth movement and ran his fingers through her damp, tangled hair.

Limp and dazed, she stared up at him blankly, slowly registering the triumphant expression in those night-black eyes as they raked her flushed cheeks.

Without shifting his gaze from hers, he reached up and freed her in one simple movement, trailing the scarlet silk ribbon that had held her captive to his sexual whims over one hardened nipple.

'*Now* you can touch me,' he informed her in silky tones and she wished she had the energy or the inclination to smack the smug smile from his indecently handsome face. He was all too aware of his own abilities to drive a woman to the edge of sanity, but unfortunately she was suffering such an overload of excitement that she could think of nothing but her own need for him.

She reached for him urgently, closing her slender fingers over the impressive throb of his erection with a moan of feminine approval.

With a grunt deep in his throat, he slid an arm under her hips, positioned her to his satisfaction and thrust deeply into her shivering, quivering body and it felt so shockingly good to have him inside her again that she gave a sob of relief. Wrapping her legs around him, she moved her hips instinctively and he muttered something against her mouth before driving into her hard and setting a rhythm that was pagan and primitive and out of control.

She raked her nails down his back and he dug his fingers into her thighs, bringing his mouth down hard on hers, connecting them in every way possible until the inevitable sensual explosion engulfed her, suspending thought and time.

Kimberley felt her mind go blank, felt her body come apart as fierce excitement gripped her. For a moment, everything was suspended and exaggerated and she struggled to breathe as her body convulsed around the plunging, primal force of his. Dimly she registered a masculine groan and knew that her climax had driven him to the same peak. She felt the liquid force of his own release, felt him thrust hard as he powered into her, felt the rasp of male chest hair against her sensitised breasts as his body moved against hers. The spasms went on and on and she clung to him, overpowered by sensation, riding the storm, waiting for the world around her to settle.

And eventually it did. Her senses cleared and calm was restored. She opened her eyes and saw a bronzed male shoulder, became aware of the slick heat of his body against hers, the harshness of his breathing against her cheek and the weight of him pressing down on her.

And then he rolled on to his back, taking her with him. Her hair tumbled and slid across his chest and he gave a satisfied groan and brushed it gently away from her face so that he could kiss her mouth.

'That was amazing.' His tone was slightly roughened and Kimberley shifted her head slightly so that she could look at him, her eyes trapped by his slumberous dark gaze. 'You are so wild in my bed. And, just in case you're tempted to pretend that you didn't enjoy it, then I ought to warn you that you'd be wasting your time,' he drawled lazily, smothering a yawn. 'You were completely mad for me and I still have the wounds on my back to prove it.'

His less than subtle reminder of just how uninhibited she'd been horrified her and she pulled away from him, suddenly realising that, despite her best intentions, he'd taken all the control right back. And, judging from the satisfied macho smile on his sickeningly handsome face, he knew it.

Ignoring the fact that her limbs felt weak and her body ached and throbbed, she sprang out of bed. It was the only way she could fight the impulse to snuggle against him. And their relationship wasn't about affection.

'Well, I thought that five million dollars required an above average performance on my part.' Her casual tone drew a quick frown from him but she turned and strolled into the bathroom with what she hoped was a convincing degree of indifference.

Inside the palatial bathroom she bolted the door and then slid in a boneless heap on to the marbled floor and covered her face with her hands.

She remembered his words as he'd untied her with a whimper of horror.

'Now you can touch me.'

Even in the middle of lovemaking, he'd still been the one in control and she'd been so desperate for him that she hadn't even noticed. In fact she'd ceased to care about anything else except satisfying the maddening, almost intolerable ache in her body. He'd orchestrated every second of her seduction, without once allowing her the same privileged, unlimited access to his body. And, although he'd clearly enjoyed their encounter, at no point in the proceedings had he appeared to lose control or been consumed by the same degree of sexual abandon.

She remembered how pleased she'd been with herself earlier when she'd taken control back for a few moments. And she remembered the surprise in his eyes. But it hadn't lasted. From the moment he'd stepped into the shower with her, he'd been in full command mode. The truth was that in the bedroom he would always be in charge. And his skills in that department were such that he could turn her into a mindless squirming mass within seconds and she just hated herself for being unable to resist him.

Dragging herself over to the mirror, she gazed at her reflection, seeing flushed cheeks and a soft, bruised mouth.

What had happened to her?

In the last seven years she'd raised a child and built a successful business from scratch. She considered herself to be competent and independent. She was proud of the woman she'd become.

And yet in Luc Santoro's bed that woman vanished and in her place was the same clingy, needy, desperate girl that she'd been at eighteen.

Two weeks, she reminded herself grimly as she splashed her face with cold water and tidied her hair. She just had to get through two weeks and then she could return home to her child and put Luc Santoro back in the past where he well and truly belonged.

CHAPTER SIX

STRETCHED out in the shade by the exquisite pool almost two weeks later, Kimberley decided drowsily that she'd undergone a complete personality change. Far from being an independent thinking woman, she now felt more like a sex slave, ready and willing to obey the commands of her master.

Luc only had to cast a burning glance in her direction and she fell into his arms with an enthusiasm as predictable as it was humiliating.

Underneath the sensual addiction that fuelled her every move she was secretly *appalled* at herself and she didn't know which was worse—the knowledge that she'd reverted to her old self the moment he'd brought his extremely talented mouth down on hers, or the fact that she was actually enjoying herself and she was far too honest a person to pretend otherwise. How could she when she couldn't take her eyes off him? *Couldn't stop wondering when he was going to reach for her next?*

If it hadn't been for the fact that she was missing Rio horribly, she would have been completely and totally happy.

Even though Luc had assured her that the money had immediately been transferred into the right account, as per her instructions, and that her surreptitious calls to Jason had assured her that everything seemed fine at home, she couldn't stop worrying.

It made no difference that she'd sneaked off at least once a day, and sometimes twice, to phone her son and chat about what was happening in his life. It made no difference that he'd sounded happy and buoyant and didn't seem to be missing her at all.

She missed him.

Desperately.

And she wanted to go home.

Which just left her to finish her part of the deal with Luc.

And so far he'd certainly been getting his money's worth. They'd barely left the bed.

Maybe it was being back in this villa, she thought helplessly as she glanced across the pool to the lush gardens that led down to the beach. It had such powerful associations with the first time they'd met that it was impossible for her to remember how much she'd changed since those days.

She'd regressed to the girl she'd been at eighteen.

'You are dreaming again.' Luc lifted himself out of the swimming pool in a lithe, powerful movement and ran a hand over his eyes to clear the water from his face. He reached for a towel and flashed her a predatory smile. 'There is no need to dream when you have the real thing. If you wish to return to the bedroom, *meu amorzinho*, then you only have to say the word.'

His arrogant assumption that her dreams had all been about him should have made her slap his face or at least deliver an acid comment about the size of his ego. But she was prevented from speaking because it was true. Her dreams *were* all about him.

And that was the most annoying thing of all, she mused as she stretched out a hand and reached for her drink. Apart from being with her child, there was no place in the world she'd rather be than in Luc's bed and she just hated herself for feeling like that. It might have been different if the relationship had been equal, but it wasn't.

He was *always* the one in control. He decided when they ate, when they slept, when they made love, even *how* they made love. Any attempt on her part to take the lead was always brushed aside.

It wasn't that Luc didn't enjoy the sex, because he clearly did, but she was humiliatingly aware that he never lost control in the way that she did. He orchestrated every move in the bedroom.

He strolled over to her, the towel looped over his broad shoulders, water clinging to the hairs on his chest and the hard muscles of his thighs. He had a body designed to scramble a woman's brain and she felt her stomach clench. No wonder she couldn't resist him. What woman could? He was as near to masculine perfection as it was possible to get.

'You've been out here for almost an hour.' He dropped the towel, a frown in his eyes as he studied her semi-naked body. 'Go back inside before you burn.'

She opened her mouth to point out that he was being controlling again, when she realised that it would give her the perfect opportunity to call home again.

She could have been open about phoning her son but, given that Luc hadn't mentioned the subject since they'd arrived on the island, it seemed more sensible to let the matter drop.

Suddenly she missed Rio so acutely that the pain was almost physical.

She needed to hear his voice.

Trying to look suitably casual, she swung her legs over the edge of the sunbed and stood up. 'You're right, I'm burning,' she stammered quickly, reaching for her bag and sliding her feet into her sandals. 'I'll go inside for a while and lie down. I'm feeling a little tired.'

It was true. Unlike Luc, who seemed possessed of almost supernatural energy levels and stamina, she found it hard to

go through an entire night with virtually no sleep without then
dropping off to sleep at various intervals throughout the day.

Ignoring the hot slide of his gaze over her body, she hur-
ried into the bedroom, reaching into her bag for her mobile
phone.

With a quick glance over her shoulder, she checked that
Luc was still safely on the terrace by the pool and then di-
alled the number.

Rio answered. 'Mum?' He sounded breathless with excitement and older than his six years. 'You have to buy me a fish!'

She closed her eyes and felt relief flood through her. He
sounded so normal. *And so like his father.* Life with Rio was
one long round of commands and orders.

'What sort of fish?'

'Like the one we've just got at school; it's *really* cool.'

Kimberley smiled. To her six-year-old son, everything was
cool.

They talked for a few more minutes and then she cut the
connection reluctantly, feeling as though she was tearing her
own heart out.

But as she dropped the phone back into her bag she saw
the letter and remembered the reason she was doing this. *She
was keeping her baby safe.*

Something glinted underneath the envelope and she gave
a slight frown and delved into the bag again, this time removing a set of handcuffs. She gave a disbelieving laugh and
then remembered that her son had borrowed a policeman's
outfit from one of his friends and had been dressing up on the
day before she'd flown out to Brazil. He must have dropped
the cuffs into her bag. How they hadn't been detected by the
airport authorities, she had no idea.

She fingered the handcuffs thoughtfully and a wickedly
naughty idea suddenly shot through her brain.

Did she dare?

Before she could lose her nerve, she quickly looped them round the bed head and covered them with a pillow.

'I've decided that I'm risking sunstroke by staying outside and that I'm also in serious need of a rest.' Luc's sardonic masculine drawl came from the doorway and she gave a start and quickly jumped off the bed, her heart thumping, convinced that the guilt must be written all over her face.

Had he noticed what she'd just done?

Her eyes clashed with his and her stomach dropped in instinctive feminine response to the masculine intent she read in his eyes. He hadn't noticed. He was too busy looking at her legs and other parts of her openly displayed by the almost non-existent bikini that had been part of her newly acquired wardrobe.

'The sun doesn't bother you and you never get tired,' she reminded him, watching him stroll towards her in a pair of swimming trunks that did nothing to conceal his rampant arousal. 'And anyway, we only got up an hour ago.'

Her mouth dried and wicked excitement curled deep in her pelvis as she stared at him helplessly.

He was unbelievably good-looking and it was no wonder he affected her so strongly.

'An hour is a long time,' he said silkily, reaching for her and dragging her to her feet. 'Especially when you are wearing that particular bikini.'

His eyes dropped to her mouth and suddenly breathing seemed difficult. 'You chose the bikini.' It had been one of a selection of clothing that had been waiting for her at the villa. 'I didn't bring any clothes, remember?'

He gave a predatory smile. 'And so far, *minha docura*, you haven't needed any.'

'When it comes to sex, you're insatiable,' she said breathlessly. 'Do you know that?'

'When it comes to *you*, I'm insatiable,' he informed her and then frowned slightly as if the thought made him uncomfortable.

'Why are you frowning?'

'I'm not.' The frown on his brow lifted as he clearly dismissed the thought with his customary single-minded determination.

She felt his hand slide down her back and gave a shiver of response. Her reaction to him was so predictable, she thought helplessly. He only had to touch her and she surrendered.

Except that this time—

He slid his hand into her hair and tugged gently, exposing the smooth skin of her neck for his touch. She gasped as she felt the burning heat of his mouth and then she was tumbled back on to the bed with Luc on top of her, his seductive gaze veiled by thick, dark lashes.

'I can't get enough of you,' he raked hoarsely as he quickly stripped her of her bikini and then fastened his mouth on hers again.

He rolled on to his back, taking her with him, and she dragged her mouth away from his. She couldn't think straight when he was kissing her. Couldn't concentrate. *And she needed to concentrate because she had a plan.*

For once she was determined to take control. She was determined to torture him the way he always tortured her.

Payback time.

Knowing that she had to act quickly, she drew his hands above his head, moving the pillow to reveal the handcuffs she'd already looped round the bed. Heart thumping, she snapped the cuffs on his wrists before he had time to realize her intentions.

He stilled and a look of stunned incredulity illuminated his dark gaze. '*What* do you think you are doing?'

She held her breath, watching as the muscles of his shoulders bunched as he jerked his wrists in an attempt to free himself. *Would the handcuffs hold?*

Deciding that she needed to use more than one method of

holding him captive, she bent her head and teased the corners
of his mouth with her tongue. 'You said you could handle me
with both hands tied behind your back,' she reminded him in
a husky voice, 'so I thought I'd give it a try. Both of your
hands are well and truly behind your back, or above your head
if you want to be precise. I'm all yours, Luc.' Her tongue slid
between his lips in a teasing, erotic gesture and she saw his
eyes darken. She lifted her head and licked her lips slowly,
savouring the taste of his mouth. 'Or perhaps you're all mine.
Let's find out, shall we?'

She saw the shock flicker across his handsome face and
for the first time in her life had the pleasure of seeing Luc
Santoro out of his depth. She saw him struggling to shake off
the raw desire so that he could think clearly and almost
smiled. *How many times had she tried to do the very same
thing in his bed and failed?*

'No woman has ever done this to you before, have they?'
She slid her body over his, soft woman over hard man, felt
the power of his erection brush against her abdomen and immediately moved away. *She wasn't ready to touch him there
yet.* 'You're about to discover what it's like to be ruled by the
senses and to be totally at the mercy of another person.'

His dark eyes were fierce. '*Meu Deus*, Kimberley. Let me
go, now!'

With agonising slowness she dragged a slender finger
through the hairs on his chest, her mouth curving into a smile
as he shuddered.

'You're not in a position to give orders,' she pointed out in
a husky voice, 'so you might just as well relax and go with
the flow. Who knows, you might find that you enjoy having
someone else in the command position for a while.'

His aggressive jaw hardened. 'Kimberley—' his tone was
hoarse and he jerked at his hands again '—I demand that you
let me go.'

'Order—' she bent her head and trailed her tongue along the hard ridge of his jaw '—demand—' her tongue snaked upwards towards his ear '—they're not the words I want to hear,' she informed him huskily, enjoying herself more and more. 'By the time I've finished with you, you're going to scream and beg, Luc. In exactly the same way that you make me scream and beg.'

'That's *different*—'

'How is it different?' She lowered her mouth again and trailed hot kisses over his bronzed muscular shoulder. *She just adored his body.* 'Because you're a man and I'm a woman?' Her teeth nipped his shoulder and she heard the hiss of his breath as he fought for control. 'You told me that you believed in equal opportunities, Luc. Let's find out whether you were telling the truth, shall we? I've just turned the tables on you.'

For the first time in their relationship she had the chance to admire his body the way he insisted on admiring hers. *She could take her time.* And she had every intention of doing just that.

Registering his stunned and slightly dazed expression with a sexy, satisfied smile, she slid her hands down his body and removed his swimming trunks in a smooth movement, sliding them down his legs and exposing him fully to her gaze.

He was hard and proud and totally ready for all the dark, sensual exploits she had in mind.

For a moment she just stared and he swore fluently in his own language and shifted his lean hips on the bed.

'Release me, now! This is *not* funny—'

'It isn't supposed to be funny.' The atmosphere in the room crackled and throbbed as the tension mounted. *He was magnificent,* she thought to herself. Hot, aroused and more of a man than he had a right to be. And she wanted him badly.

But she was going to make herself wait.

And, more to the point, she was going to make *him* wait.

With a low laugh of triumph and a heated glance that was pure seductress, she slid her fingers down his body until her hand lingered teasingly on his taut abdomen, just short of the straining shaft of his manhood.

'Release me!' He swore softly and pulled hard at the handcuffs but they held firm and Kimberley lifted her head and smiled a womanly smile, her confidence and power increasing by the minute.

'No way.' Her hand slid to the top of his thigh. 'For once I've got you exactly where I want you and you're going to stay there until I've finished with you.'

'You can't do this—'

'I *am* doing it. It's time you learned that you can't always be the one in control. I'm going to show you what it feels like to be tortured by sensual pleasure.'

He gave a soft curse and jerked at the handcuffs again but still they held fast and Kimberley bent her head, her glorious fiery hair trailing over his body as she used her tongue to trace the line of hair that ran below his navel. Her touch was slow and teasing and she saw the muscles of his abdomen tense viciously. He wanted her to touch him, badly, but she was determined not to. Not yet. She wasn't ready. And neither was he.

She had never been given unrestricted access to his body before and suddenly she needed to touch and taste all of him. To know him in every way possible.

Dimly she heard the harshness of his breathing, but she was too caught up in the sensual feast she'd made for herself to be distracted. She licked and nibbled and tasted him everywhere except his throbbing, pulsing masculinity.

Once, her fingers brushed against him fleetingly and she heard his guttural groan and felt him jerk his body towards her but she pulled back and slid up his body, raking her fingers through his chest hair and using her tongue to tease his nipples.

His breathing was harsh in her ears and she saw the muscles in his shoulders bunch as he pulled at the restraints, but he failed to free himself and cursed again, his eyes burning dark in his handsome face.

He muttered something in his own language and she lifted her head and gave him a mocking smile.

'If you expect me to understand what you're saying, you're going to have to speak English.' Her voice was smoky and softened by desire. 'What is it you want, Luc?'

For a moment he just stared at her, obviously unable to form the words, his eyes glazed and fevered. Then he licked his tongue over his lips. 'I want you to touch me,' he muttered hoarsely. 'Touch me now.'

There was no mistaking just how much he wanted her and she felt a flash of womanly triumph. 'Not yet. I'm not ready, and neither are you.'

He closed his eyes and beads of sweat appeared on his brow. 'Kimberley, please—'

A feeling of power spread through her veins and she gave a slow womanly smile. 'When I'm ready, I'll touch you,' she told him in a husky, smoky voice. 'All you have to do is lie there.' She shifted up the bed and teased the corner of his mouth with her tongue. Instantly he moved his mouth to capture hers but she was too quick for him, moving just out of reach and smiling as he swore fluently.

'This isn't a joke, Kimberley!'

'I know that. I never joke about sex.' She saw from the flash in his eyes that he recognised the words that he'd spoken to her. 'Just relax, Luc. It may have escaped your notice, but this time *I'm* the one in control. I've got you exactly where I want you and you're not going anywhere until I've finished with you.'

He swore under his breath but she saw him harden still further and gave a low laugh of satisfaction. He wanted her every bit as much as she wanted him and the knowledge thrilled her. Suddenly aware of her own power, she raked a nail down his chest and ran her tongue over her lips.

'I'm going to make you sob and beg, Luc,' she said softly, leaning forward and tracing the line of his rough jaw with her tongue. 'I'm going to make you so desperate that you can't even remember who you are or what you're doing here.'

She slid a hand slowly down his taut body and rested her palm just millimetres away from his straining manhood.

His hard jaw clenched and his eyes glittered dangerously. 'I will make you suffer for this.'

'You're the one who's suffering, Luc.'

But the truth was that she was suffering too. Her body ached and throbbed with a need that she hadn't experienced before. She was supposed to be the one doing the seducing but having his perfect masculine physique stretched out for her enjoyment was a temptation too great to resist.

She proceeded to lick her way down his body, exploring him everywhere except that one place that was straining to be touched. Her long hair fell forward, sliding over his naked, straining body like a sensual cloak.

'Kimberley—' His hoarse plea made her lift her head and she gazed at him, her mouth damp and her eyes shimmering with need.

'Not yet ' Desire curled low in her pelvis but she held it in check, determined to delay his satisfaction the way he always delayed hers. 'You haven't begged.'

'*Meu Deus*—' he cursed softly and closed his eyes, thick dark lashes brushing his bronzed skin as he struggled against his body's natural desire for satisfaction.

Her gaze slid down his body and her mouth dried. He was rock-hard and so aroused that she felt her mouth dry in anticipation. Why hadn't she thought of doing this before? she wondered.

For the first time she felt strong and powerful.

For the first time she felt like his equal.

For the first time she was able to torment him the way he always took pleasure in tormenting her.

She waited until every muscle was straining in his powerful body, until she couldn't wait any longer.

'Kimberley—' His voice shook and his lean hips thrust upwards. 'I'm begging—'

And then she touched him.

With the hot slide of her mouth, she took him and tasted, his harsh moans of pleasure fuelling her own sense of power and need. She explored every part of him with her fingers, with her tongue until she could no longer bear the ache deep in her body.

Only then did she lift her head and slide on top of him. She positioned herself over him, her hair trailing over his chest, her eyes fixed on his face as she allowed only the tip of his manhood to touch her intimately. With a soft curse he strained upwards trying to fill her, trying to take her breast in his mouth, but she held herself slightly away from him and leaned forward to kiss him.

'I'm still the one in control, Luc,' she whispered against his lips, but she knew that, strictly speaking, it wasn't true. She wanted him every bit as desperately as he wanted her.

But still she was going to make him wait.

She made him wait until the beads of sweat gathered on his brow, until he could no longer see straight, *until she wanted him so badly that she couldn't hold herself back a moment longer.*

And then finally she took him. Deep inside her so that she could feel the hard throb of his erection with every pulse of her body, so that she forgot that they were supposed to be separate, man and woman. Instead they were one.

And when the inevitable explosion came it was so blisteringly intense that for a moment she was afraid of what she'd unleashed. It was a beast that couldn't be tamed. A beast that savaged both of them. A beast that had to be allowed to run riot until finally it burned itself out.

Which it finally did. In a riot of soft cries, harsh groans, gasps and sobs and slippery flesh, the beast finally left them.

Struggling to breathe, Kimberley slid sideways, her arm over his chest, her leg over his leg.

Eventually her senses settled and she dared to lift her head.

He lay with his eyes closed, dense dark lashes brushing his perfect bone structure, his arms still locked above his head.

Suddenly, in the aftermath of such intimacy, she felt ridiculously shy and self-conscious. 'Luc?'

He didn't respond and she gave a frown and reached up and undid the handcuffs.

Instantly strong arms came around her and he rolled her on to her back, his eyes burning into hers. 'I can't believe you just did that—'

She felt the power and strength of his body pressing into her and gave a soft gasp. 'Are you angry with me?'

'Angry?' He groaned and brushed his mouth over hers in a lingering kiss. 'How could I be angry with you for giving me the best sex of my life? And anyway I don't have the energy to be angry. I don't have the energy for anything.'

She smiled, feeling clever and beautiful and every inch a woman. 'It was good, wasn't it?'

He rolled on to his back, taking her with him. 'It was amazing,' he said huskily, stroking her tangled hair away from her flushed cheeks with a gentle hand. 'Where did you get those handcuffs?'

She tensed. That was a question she hadn't anticipated and she didn't want to spoil the moment by mentioning Rio. 'Someone I know was playing a joke on me,' she muttered vaguely, hoping that he wouldn't delve further.

Fortunately he didn't. Instead he hauled her closer still, snuggling her against him.

She felt a flicker of surprise. Luc tolerated a cuddle after sex but she could never recall him initiating that kind of contact before.

Luc did sex. He didn't do the emotional stuff.

He kissed the top of her head. 'I can't believe you just did that. And I can't believe I just let you.'

She gave a low laugh, more than a little pleased with herself. 'You didn't have any choice. For the first time in your life, you weren't the one in control. I was.'

To her surprise, he laughed. 'You're right, you are a different woman now,' he said in husky tones as he slid a hand over her heated flesh with undisguised masculine appreciation. 'You never would have had the courage to do what you just did seven years ago. In fact, you were pretty shocked by me.'

'You were my first lover,' she reminded him. 'I hadn't done any of those things before and you were totally controlling.'

'Necessary,' he assured her arrogantly, 'because you were too tied up with your inhibitions to let go. You were only able to do so when you could convince yourself that I was the one who seduced you. It was all my fault, isn't that right, *meu amorzinho*?'

There was laughter in his voice and she lifted her head and gave him a reproachful look. 'I was a virgin.'

He gave a macho, self-satisfied smile. 'I *know* that. And being the only man who had ever slept with you gave me an incredible high. Now, go to sleep.' He tightened his grip. 'You need to get some rest and recover your energy.'

Having delivered that command, he closed his eyes and promptly fell asleep himself, his arms locked firmly around her.

And it felt so good that Kimberley hardly dared move in case he woke up and changed his mind about the cuddle.

Being held by him made her feel safe and secure. *And it felt totally right.*

Which was ridiculous, she told herself, because there was nothing right about a relationship based on nothing more than sex.

Slowly, the happiness drained out of her as realisation dawned.

For her it was so much more than sex, and it always had been. She'd dismissed what she'd felt for him at eighteen as childish infatuation. Who wouldn't have been dazzled by a man as sophisticated as Luc? But the truth was that she'd loved Luc almost from the first moment she'd set eyes on him and time had done nothing to dilute her feelings. What she'd felt as a girl was no different to what she felt now, as a woman. Love was the reason she was so vulnerable to Luc. Love was the reason she hadn't looked at another man in the last seven years. It didn't matter that he was controlling and that he revealed nothing of himself. *It didn't matter that he was totally the wrong man.*

It didn't even matter that he didn't love her.

She still loved him.

She closed her eyes tightly, refusing to allow her bleak thoughts to spoil the moment. It would be over soon enough because they were almost at the end of their two weeks.

Luc woke several hours later to find the sun setting and Kimberley gone.

He felt a flicker of something that he didn't recognise. *Disappointment*, he decided immediately, rejecting the opportunity to examine his emotions in more detail.

The most explosive sex of his entire life had left him feeling refreshed and invigorated and more than ready to appreciate the woman who had been part of the experience.

Was it surprising that he felt disappointed that she wasn't still lying in his arms?

He sprang out of bed, noted the abandoned handcuffs with an appreciative male smile, and reached for a pair of casual trousers.

He found her by the pool, her expression pale and strained, her mobile phone in her hand.

The tension in her slender frame stopped him dead. 'Is something wrong?'

After what they'd shared, he'd expected to find her relaxed and smiling, recovering her energy levels in the sun, ready for the next bout of lovemaking. Instead she gave a start and shot him a guilty look before stuffing the phone back in her bag. 'Nothing's wrong.'

More unfamiliar emotions boiled up inside him. 'Who were you calling?'

She dipped her head, her long fiery hair concealing her expression from him. 'Just a friend.'

A friend?

Luc felt the sharp claws of jealousy dig into his flesh. What sex was the 'friend'? Had she been talking to another man? What was her life like when she was at home? Did she date? *Had she tied another man to the bed and rendered him unable to think?*

He realised with no small degree of discomfort that, although he'd spent weeks in bed with this woman, he knew next to nothing about her, and suddenly he was driven by a burning desire to discover *everything*.

'We're dining on the terrace tonight,' he said firmly as she glanced up at him, clearly as startled by hearing this unusual announcement as he had felt making it. 'And we're going to talk.'

She blinked and her lips parted. Those perfectly shaped lips that had driven him wild only hours earlier.

Resolutely Luc pushed the thought away. He wasn't going to think about that now. The same instincts that had made him an unbeatable force in business were currently telling him that something wasn't right about this situation. And he intended to make it right. He had a sudden burning need to see her smiling again. The reason *why* he should suddenly feel the urge to make a woman happy outside the bedroom didn't occur to him as he searched his brain for an answer.

Obviously she wasn't short of sex, so the problem couldn't possibly lie there. Just to confirm that fact, his mind ran speedily through the time they'd spent together and he concluded with a warm feeling of masculine satisfaction that she *definitely* couldn't be feeling unappreciated in that department.

Which meant that the problem must lie elsewhere.

Romance.

With a sudden burst of clarity, he identified the reason for her long face.

Perhaps the last two weeks had been a little too bedroom focused, he conceded. Wasn't it true that women needed different things to men? Apparently whole books had been written on the subject. For some inexplicable reason women needed to *talk* and certainly during the past two weeks he and Kimberley hadn't indulged much in the way of conversation. Acknowledgment of that fact would normally have left him nothing short of indifferent, but for some reason that he didn't entirely understand he suddenly felt a driving need to give her everything she wanted. *He wanted to make Kimberley happy.* And if conversation was what it took, then he was willing to make that sacrifice.

Convinced that he'd found the solution to the white, pinched look on her face, he waved a hand towards the bedroom with the smug look of a man who knew he had all the answers when it came to women.

'There are clothes in the wardrobe,' he informed her silkily. 'Choose something and meet me out here when you're dressed.'

She stared at him blankly, as if he'd just delivered a command that was nothing short of incomprehensible.

'What's the point of getting dressed when you're just going to strip me naked again?' she asked him and there was a hint of wariness in her tone that triggered his male early warning system.

Telling himself that he could exercise restraint when there was a higher purpose, he gave a smile. 'Because tonight I'm more interested in your mind than your body. We're going to *talk, meu amorzinho,* and I'm going to find out everything there is to know about you.'

That soft mouth, *the same mouth that had taken him to paradise and back,* curved into a wry smile. 'And what about you, Luc? Are you going to talk too? Or am I going to be the one doing all the giving? Perhaps I want to know everything there is to know about you too.'

Luc gave a brief frown but recovered himself in time. If she wanted him to talk too, then he could do that. True, it wasn't his favourite pastime, but he dealt with inquisitive journalists on a daily basis and was used to talking about a wide range of subjects. He was more than confident that he could maintain conversation over dinner with an attractive woman if the incentive was great enough.

'I look forward to telling you everything you want to know,' he said diplomatically, urging her back towards the villa with the palm of his hand. 'Change and I'll ask the staff to serve dinner by the pool.'

She walked away from him with the fluid, graceful movement of a dancer. Luc's eyes automatically slid down her slender back and he struggled briefly against a powerful impulse to forget this whole 'romantic' approach and indulge the caveman that was threatening to burst out from inside him.

Remembering the desolate expression on her face, he reminded himself that a small investment could often yield surprising results and that might well be the case with Kimberley.

He was entirely confident that exercising physical restraint for a short time would pay dividends in the bedroom.

All he needed to make his investment complete were pretty flowers, good wine and plenty of delicious food and the smile would soon be back on her face.

Easy, he thought to himself as he strode purposefully towards the kitchen to brief his chef and his housekeeper. Handling women was no different from any other business negotiation. It was just a question of identifying their weakness, and then moving in for the kill.

Before the evening was out, she'd be smiling again.

And he could satisfy the caveman inside him.

CHAPTER SEVEN

'SO WHY did you give up modelling?'

Luc lounged across from her, his face bronzed and lethally handsome in the flickering candlelight. The setting couldn't have been more romantic. The pool was illuminated by what seemed like hundreds of tiny lights, the evening was warm and the air was filled with the heady scent of exotic flowers. It was a setting fit for seduction and yet he'd already seduced her. More times than she cared to count.

So why the exotic arrangement of flowers on the table?

Why the tablecloth and the sparkling crystal?

And why was he dressed in a pair of tailored trousers and an exquisite silk shirt when he'd barely bothered to get dressed for the past two weeks?

If it hadn't been Luc sitting across from her, she would have thought that the setting had been designed for romance.

But Luc didn't do romantic. Luc did white-hot sex. Luc did blistering, uncontrollable passion. Luc did control and domination. He most certainly, *definitely* didn't do romantic.

So why was he doing it now?

And why the sudden desire to acquaint himself with her every thought and feeling? Ever since she'd emerged on to the terrace he'd been openly solicitous about every aspect of her comfort and asked her endless questions about herself until she felt like a candidate in an interview. Especially because it was impossible to relax in case she gave the wrong answers and revealed too much.

Kimberley concentrated on her food, wondering what had sparked Luc's sudden uncharacteristic desire for conversation. Had he guessed that she was hiding something? Had he overheard her on the phone?

'Modelling gave me up,' she said dryly, 'when I chose not to turn up for any of the swimwear shots on the beach because I was in your bed. It was a lucrative account for the agency and I lost it for them. They took me off their books and made sure I wasn't given work again.'

Luc's eyes hardened. 'Give me the name of the agency.'

She blinked. 'Why?' Amusement lit her eyes. 'Are you going to close them down?'

He didn't smile. 'Maybe.'

'There's no need. I was glad to give up modelling. The lifestyle never suited me. You know I was never comfortable with the partying, the drugs—any of that.'

'I know you were incredibly naïve and innocent when I met you,' he drawled softly, leaning across to top up her glass. 'Why else would you have been walking along the beach in Rio de Janeiro at midnight in a non existent dress with your hair dazzling like an Olympic torch? I couldn't believe my eyes. You were like some sort of virgin sacrifice, left out for the lions to consume.'

She gave a wry smile, acknowledging how stupid she'd been. 'The other girls persuaded me to go to a party but I hated every moment. I just wanted to get back to my hotel and there were no taxis,' she said simply, remembering that evening with a small shudder. If Luc hadn't come along when he had—

'It had been a long time since I'd been required to test my skills against a flick-knife,' Luc observed lightly, his eyes rest-ing on her face in an intense male scrutiny that she found more than a little disturbing.

'You were impressive,' she conceded, wondering if the moment when he'd taken on a gang of six thugs, all with knives, had been when she'd fallen in love with him.

But even dressed in a shockingly expensive designer suit Luc Santoro looked like a man who could handle himself. And she'd be less than honest if she didn't admit that his spontaneous demonstration of physical skill and courage had been one of the elements that had initially drawn her to him. When in her life, before that moment, had anyone ever defended her? Never, and the novelty of meeting a man prepared to risk his life to extract a female from a situation that had been entirely of her own making had proved more than a little intoxicating.

In the single second it had taken him to identify the leader of the gang, he'd moved with such speed and skill that Kimberley had wondered for a moment whether her rescuer might not be more dangerous than her attackers.

Where exactly had he learned those street-fighting tactics that he'd used to extricate her from danger that night?

Kimberley fingered her glass and glanced across at him, remembering the gossip that she'd heard about his past. Nothing specific. Just speculation.

Her eyes hovered on his blue-shadowed jaw and the hard male perfection of his bone structure. No one with a grain of common sense would mess with Luc Santoro.

'Where did you learn to fight?' She asked the question before she could stop herself and she saw his hand still en route to his glass.

'*Não entendo.* I don't understand.' He frowned at her. 'What do you mean, "fight"?'

She swallowed. 'The night you rescued me, you took on six men. How did you learn to do that? *Where* did you learn?'

He picked up his glass. 'I'm a man. Fighting is instinctive.'

'I don't believe that.' Something made her push the point. 'You were outnumbered six to one and you anticipated all their tricks. As if you'd been trained in the same school of fighting.'

There was the briefest pause. 'The school of fighting I attended is called life,' he said dryly. 'I learned a great deal and I learned it early on.'

'What was it about your life that made it necessary for you to learn those skills? I've never learned them. If I had, perhaps I wouldn't have got myself into trouble that night,' she admitted. 'I wasn't very streetwise. To be honest, there wasn't any need to be where I was brought up.'

He gave a short laugh and drank deeply. 'You once told me that your home was a leafy English village where everyone knew everyone. Very middle class. Perhaps it's hardly surprising that you didn't find yourself learning self-defence.'

Maybe that was why he fascinated her. He was a man of contradictions. On the one hand he had great wealth and sophistication and he moved in the highest, most glittering social circles. But that veneer of sophistication didn't entirely hide the dark, dangerous, almost primitive side of his nature that she'd sensed from the very first moment they'd met. There was nothing tame or safe about Luc Santoro.

Which was one of the reasons he was so irresistible to women

'I take it your upbringing wasn't middle class,' she ventured. 'Were you born in Rio de Janeiro?'

'Yes.' His smile was slightly mocking. 'I'm a genuine *Carioca*.'

She knew that was the name given to someone born or living in Rio de Janeiro.

'So how did you make it from *Carioca* to billionaire tycoon?' she asked lightly and he delivered her a smile that both charmed and seduced.

'Motivation and hard work.' He leaned forward, his eyes fixed on her face. 'If you want something badly enough, *meu amorzinho*, you can have it. It's just a question of careful planning and letting nothing stand in your way.'

His cold, ruthless approach to life, so different from her own, made her shiver. 'Just because you want something you can't just go out there and take it!'

His gaze didn't shift from hers. 'Why not?'

'Because you have to consider other people.'

A slightly mocking smile touched his beautifully shaped mouth. 'That's a typically female approach.' The smile faded. 'I, on the other hand, believe that trusting people is a hobby for fools. You decide what you want in life and then you go for it. You build something up until no one can take it away from you.'

There was such passion and volatility in the sudden flash of his dark eyes that Kimberley found that she was holding her breath. For one brief tantalising moment she felt she'd been given a glimpse of the real Luc—the man underneath that cool, emotionless exterior.

Sensing the sudden turbulence in his mood, she reached across the table in an instinctive gesture of comfort. 'Is that what happened?' Her voice was soft. 'Did someone take something away from you?'

He removed his hand from hers and leaned back in his chair, dark eyes veiled. 'Why do women always search for the dramatic? Everyone's character is formed by events in their lives.' He gave a dismissive shrug. 'I'm no different.'

'But you shut everyone out,' she said passionately and he gave a cool smile.

'I'm a man, *meu amorzinho*, and like most men I hunt alone. And I don't allow another male to poach on my territory. The friend you were speaking to earlier—' the warmth of his tone dropped several degrees '—was it a man?'

His slick change of subject took her by surprise and she answered without thinking. 'Yes.'

She saw his eyes glint dangerously and his lean, strong fingers tighten on his glass. Suddenly the atmosphere changed from comfortable to menacing.

His mouth was set in a grim line and his body held a certain stillness that raised the tension several notches. 'And have you been together long?'

'It isn't like that—'

'Evidently not,' he delivered with ruthless bite, 'if he allows his woman to spend two weeks in another man's bed. Or doesn't he know?'

She bit her lip. 'He's just a friend—'

'How good a friend?'

'The very best!' Loyalty to Jason made her tell the truth. 'He's stood by me through everything.'

'I'm sure he's done far more than stand.' The sardonic lift of his dark brow stung her more than his sarcasm.

She dropped her fork with a clatter. 'Not everyone is like you, Luc! Some people have proper relationships.' She rose to her feet, so angry and upset that she almost knocked the chair over. 'Relationships that aren't all about sex and nothing else. But you're so emotionally stunted you couldn't possibly understand that.'

'*Mou Dous*, what is this about?' He rose to his feet too, six-foot-four of powerful, angry male. Tension throbbed and pulsed between them. 'I am *not* emotionally stunted.'

She lifted her hands in a gesture of exasperation. 'Then *tell* me something about yourself! Anything.'

'Why? What does the sharing of past history bring to a relationship?' His eyes burned dark with temper. 'Does it change things between us if I tell you that I was born in the *favelas*, the slums of Rio, so poor that food was a luxury? Does it change things between us if I tell you that my father and mother worked like animals to take themselves and me away from that place? *Does it help you to know that they succeeded, only to lose everything and be forced back into the lifestyle they'd fought so hard to leave behind?'* He paced round the table and dragged her hard against him, his face grim and set as he raked her shocked face with night-black eyes. 'Tell me, *meu amorzinho*, now that you know the truth of where I came from, now that you know that I have emotions, has our relationship improved?'

Somehow she found her voice. 'That's the first time you've ever told me anything about yourself.'

'Then savour the moment,' he advised silkily, raking lean bronzed fingers through her silky hair in an unmistakably possessive gesture, 'because mindless chatter about past events doesn't rank as my favourite pastime.'

Had she been in any doubt, one breathless glance into his dark eyes enlightened her as to exactly what constituted his favourite pastime.

'I thought tonight was about conversation and getting to know each other.'

'You now know more about me than almost any other person on the planet,' he delivered in husky tones, tugging at her hair gently and fastening his mouth on the smooth pale skin of her neck. 'Let's leave it at that.'

His tongue flickered and teased and she felt her stomach shift and her eyes drifted closed. 'Luc—'

'A man can only stand so much talking in one night,' he groaned against her skin, sliding his hand down her back and bringing her hard against him. 'It's time to revert to body language.'

With that he scooped her up and carried her through to the bedroom.

She stared up at him in a state of helpless excitement, part of her simmering with exasperation that his ability to sustain a conversation about himself had been so short-lived and part of her as desperate for him as he clearly was for her.

They'd made progress, she thought, as he stripped off his shirt and dropped it on the floor with indecent haste and a careless disregard for its future appearance. Small progress, perhaps, but still, it was progress.

They'd dressed. They'd shared a meal. They'd talked—sort of.

And that was her last coherent thought as he stripped her naked with ruthless precision and brought his mouth down on hers.

Kimberley waited for all the usual feelings to swamp her but this time something was different. He was different. More gentle. More caring?

The thought popped into her head and she pushed it away ruthlessly. No! She wasn't going to do that again—make the mistake of believing that Luc was interested in anything other than her body. She'd done that once before and allowing herself to dream about something that could never happen had almost broken her heart.

But it *was* different.

Instead of dominating or being dominated, they *shared* and when they finally descended from an explosive climax he held her firmly against him, refusing to let her go.

As the delicious spasms died and they both lay spent and exhausted, he still refused to let her go, curving her into his body and locking his arms tightly around her as if he was afraid she might leave.

Which was ridiculous, she told herself sleepily, because they both knew that she was leaving and they both knew he wouldn't care.

The two weeks was almost up.

But she was too sleepy to make sense of any of it and eventually she stopped wondering and asking herself questions and drifted off to sleep in the warm, safe circle of his arms.

The day before she was due to fly home, Kimberley awoke late and found the bed empty.

Her heart gave a thud of disappointment and then she noticed that the French doors on to the terrace were open and she heard the rhythmic splashing of someone swimming in the pool.

She lay there and smiled.

Obviously Luc had decided on an early swim. Or maybe not that early, she thought ruefully as she cast a glance at her watch.

Now would be a good time to phone home for the final time, to check on the arrangements for the following day.

She scraped her tangled hair out of her eyes, flinched slightly as her bruised aching body reminded her of how they'd spent most of the night, and reached for her phone.

Jason answered and they talked for a bit and then she spoke to Rio, a soft smile touching her mouth as she listened to his excited chatter.

She couldn't wait to see him.

'I miss you, baby.'

'Are you coming home soon, Mummy?' Suddenly he sounded very young. 'I miss you.'

Tears clogged her throat. 'I'll be home tomorrow. And I miss you too.'

She heard a noise behind her and, with a horrified premonition, she turned round to see Luc standing there. A towel was looped carelessly around his waist, his breathtakingly gorgeous bronzed body was glistening with water and his expression black as thunder.

She said a hasty goodbye to Rio, cut the connection and turned to face the music.

'So your *"friend"* is missing you.' His tone was icy cold

as he padded towards her, all simmering anger and lethal menace. 'Next time you can tell the "*friend*" that he's poaching on my time.'

She couldn't understand why he was so angry.

'Our two weeks are up tomorrow, Luc,' she reminded him, trying to keep her tone reasonable, 'and I was making arrangements.'

He stopped dead and stared at her blankly, as if she'd told him something that he didn't already know. Something flitted across his handsome face. Surprise? Regret?

'It was just a phone call—' If she hadn't known better she would have said that he was jealous, but how could he be jealous of a phone call?

For a moment her heart skittered slightly and then she remembered that in order to be jealous you had to care, and Luc didn't care about anything except sex. He enjoyed the physical side of their relationship but nothing more.

'This is ridiculous,' she said, trying to keep her voice steady. 'You were the one who negotiated the terms. You agreed to two weeks, Luc, and those two weeks are up today.'

'I didn't agree to two weeks. You really can't wait to get home to him, can you?'

She gaped at him in disbelief. 'Why are you behaving like this? It doesn't make sense. Especially as we don't even have a proper relationship.'

His breath hissed through his teeth. 'We *do* have a relationship. What do you think the last two weeks have been all about?'

'Sex,' she replied in a flat tone. 'The last two weeks have been all about sex.'

The anger faded and he eyed her warily, like a man who knew he was on extremely rocky ground. '*Not* just about sex. Last night we talked.'

'*I* talked,' she pointed out wryly. '*You* questioned me.'

His hard jaw clenched. 'I told you about my past.'

'You yelled and shouted and lost your temper,' she reminded him in a calm voice, 'and then reluctantly disclosed a tiny morsel of your experiences in childhood! Prisoners under torture have revealed more!'

'Well, I'm not *used* to talking about myself,' he exclaimed defensively, pacing across the floor and throwing her a simmering black look. 'But if that's what you want, we'll have dinner on the terrace again tonight and we'll talk again.'

She stared at him, stunned into silence by his uncharacteristic offer to do something that was so completely against his nature.

Why would he bother?

'I have to go home, Luc,' she said quietly and he stopped pacing and simply glared at her.

'*Why?*'

'Because I have a child,' she said flatly, 'a child who I love and miss and need to be near. We've carefully avoided mentioning it for the past two weeks but the fact that we haven't mentioned it doesn't change the facts. My *life* is in London and tomorrow I'm going home.'

A muscle flickered in his lean jaw. 'You have a *lover* in London.'

Was he ignoring the issue of Rio once again?

She rose to her feet, totally bemused. 'Why are you acting in this jealous, possessive fashion when we both knew that this was just for two weeks?'

'I'm *not* jealous,' he refuted her accusation in proud tones, the disdainful look he cast in her direction telling her exactly what he thought of the mere suggestion that he might suffer from such a base emotion. 'But I don't share. Ever. I told you that once before.'

Kimberley closed her eyes briefly and decided that if she

lived to be a hundred and read every book written on the subject, she'd never understand men.

'My flight leaves tomorrow afternoon,' she reminded him steadily and his eyes narrowed.

'Cancel that flight,' he advised silkily, 'or I will cancel it for you.'

She'd done it again, she thought helplessly as she dragged her eyes away from his magnificent body. Given herself to him, heart, body and soul. And now she was going to have to find a way to recover.

How could she ever have thought she'd be able to walk away from him and feel nothing?

They had clinics for coming off drugs and drinks, she reflected with almost hysterical amusement. What she needed was a clinic for breaking her addiction to Luciano Santoro. Otherwise she was going to live the rest of her life craving a man she couldn't have.

Jealous?

Luc powered through the swimming pool yet again in an attempt to drive out the uncomfortable and unfamiliar thoughts and feelings that crowded his brain. The fact that he'd spent an unusual amount of time in the pool in pursuit of calm that continued to elude him hadn't escaped him.

If he was totally honest, then he didn't exactly know what was happening to him at the moment. Certainly he'd never felt the same burning need to keep a woman by his side as he did with Kimberley.

But was that really so surprising? he reasoned. She was *incredible* in bed. What normal sane man would want to let her go? It had nothing to do with jealousy and everything to do with sanity, he decided as he executed a perfect turn and swam down the pool again.

The fact that the agreed two weeks hadn't been enough to

get her out of his system troubled him slightly, but he was entirely sure that a week or two more would be sufficient to convince him of the merits of moving on to another willing female, this time someone less motivated to discover everything about him.

He'd simply work out a way of persuading Kimberley to extend their deal, he decided, confident that the problem was now all but solved.

With his usual limitless energy, he sprang out of the pool and reached for a towel.

The fact that she appeared to be determined to fly home the following day didn't trouble him in the slightest. He would simply talk her out of it. How hard could that be for a man who negotiated million dollar deals before breakfast on virtually a daily basis? He dealt with hard-nosed businessmen all the time. One extremely willing woman would be a piece of cake, even if she did have red hair, an extremely uncertain temper and what could almost be termed as a conversation disorder.

He had one more night.

He'd start by proving to her that he could talk as much as the next man when the situation called for it. Then he'd take her to bed.

By the end of the night he was entirely confident that she would be the one calling the airline to cancel her flight.

The following morning Kimberley checked her flight ticket and her passport and tucked them carefully back into her handbag. A small piece of hand luggage lay open on the bed. She'd found the case in her dressing room and, since it was clearly for her use and the clothes had been purchased specifically for her, she'd decided that she might as well take her favourites. Probably none of Luc's other girlfriends ever wore the same outfit twice, she thought wryly as she slipped the silk dress off the hanger and placed it carefully in the case, trying not to think too hard about what leaving would mean.

The previous evening they'd dined on the terrace again, and this time Luc had made what could only be described as a heroic effort to talk about himself. In fact he hadn't stopped talking and if she hadn't been so touched she would have laughed.

It was such an obvious struggle for him to discuss anything remotely personal but he'd tried extremely hard, sharing with her all manner of snippets about his childhood and the way his office worked.

The question of *why* he was trying so hard slid into her mind, but she dismissed it because the answer was so obvious. He wanted her to stay because he wanted more sex and for some reason he'd worked out that the way to change her mind about leaving was to start talking.

But of course her mind hadn't been changed, even by what had followed. Before last night she'd thought that she'd already experienced the very best in sex. But Luc had been relentless in his determination to drive her to the very pinnacle of ecstasy, proving once again that he was a skilled and sophisticated lover.

And she couldn't imagine living without him.

She was *desperate* to go home and be with her son, but she wanted to be with Luc too.

At that moment he walked out from the bathroom, his dark jaw freshly shaved, his hair still damp from the shower. Despite his almost total absence of sleep, he looked refreshed and invigorated and sexier than any man had a right to be.

Her eyes feasted on him, knowing that it would probably be the last time.

If she didn't have her son to think of, would she have stayed?

No, because she wasn't going to get her heart broken a second time in her life, she told herself firmly as she dropped a bikini into the case.

His gaze fastened on the case and he gave a sharp frown. 'Why are you packing?'

'Because I'm going home,' she reminded him, slightly bemused by his question. He knew she was going home that afternoon. 'I'm presuming your pilot will take me to the airport.'

'He certainly will not.' The Rolex on his bronzed wrist glinted as he reached out to remove the bag from her hand in a decisive movement. 'Because you're not going home. I thought we both agreed that.'

Kimberley racked her brain and tried to recall having said anything that might have given him that impression. 'We didn't agree that.'

He stepped closer to her and slid a possessive hand into her hair. 'Did we or did we not,' he enquired in silky tones, 'spend the entire night making love?'

Her face heated at the memory and the breath caught in her throat. 'Yes, but—'

His dark head lowered towards hers, an arrogant smile on his sexy mouth. 'And was it, or was it not, the most mindblowing experience of your life?'

The flames flickered higher and higher inside her. 'It was amazing,' she agreed huskily, 'but I still have to go.'

The arrogant smile faded and blank incomprehension flickered across his handsome face. 'Why?'

'Because I have to go home.'

His brow cleared. 'Easily solved. Your home is now here. With me.'

She stared at him in amazement and a flicker of crazy hope came to life inside her. 'You want me to live with you?' She was so stunned that her voice cracked and he gave a smile loaded with an abundance of male self-confidence.

'Of course. The sex between us is simply amazing. I'd have to be out of my mind to let you go. So you stay. As my mistress. Until we decide that we've had enough of each other.'

The hope disintegrated into a million tiny pieces, blown away by his total lack of sensitivity, and she stared at him in disbelief.

'Your *mistress?* Are we suddenly living in the Middle Ages?'

'Mistress, girlfriend—' He gave a casual lift of his broad shoulders to indicate that he considered the terms both interchangeable and irrelevant. 'Choose whatever title you like.'

'How about "mug" or "idiot"?' Kimberley suggested helpfully, her temper starting to boil, 'because that's what I'd be if I accepted an invitation like that from a man like you.'

How could she have allowed herself to think for one single solitary minute that he might care for her just a little bit?

Luc wasn't capable of caring for anyone.

He raked long fingers through his dark hair, his expression showing that he was holding on to his patience with visible effort. 'I don't think you understood,' he said stiffly. 'I'm suggesting that you move in with me on a permanent basis, at least for the foreseeable future—'

'That's semi-permanent, Luc, and I understood you perfectly. Sex on tap, until I bore you.' Kimberley reached for the nightdress she'd worn before he'd stripped it from her quivering, pliant body. 'Very convenient for you—very precarious for me. So no thanks. These days I have more self-respect than to accept an offer like that.' She stuffed the nightdress in the case, as angry with herself as she was with him.

How could she have been so stupid as to fall for this man again?

How could she have been that shallow?

'*No thanks?*' Night-black eyes raked her flushed cheeks

with a lethal mixture of naked incredulity and stunned amazement. 'Do you realise that I have never made that offer to a woman before in my entire life? I will need to start visiting the office occasionally but believe me, *meu amorzinho*, we will be spending plenty of time together.' His voice dropped to a sexy drawl as he clearly dismissed her refusal as a misunderstanding. 'From now on I'll be extremely motivated to finish my working day early.'

Clearly he thought that was sufficient inducement for her to empty the contents of the case back into the drawers.

'You're unbelievable, do you know that?' She stared at him with a mixture of amazement and exasperation, wondering whether a sharp blow to the head would be of any help in bringing him to his senses. 'It is *not* a compliment to know that someone wants you just for sex!'

He frowned. 'If you're pretending the sex isn't amazing between us then you're deluding yourself again and I thought we'd moved past that point.'

'There's nothing wrong with the sex. The sex is great. The sex is amazing.' She spoke in staccato tones as she turned back to the bed and continued to stuff and push things into the tiny bag. 'But there are other things that are just as important as sex and there's *everything* wrong with those.'

'What do you mean, other things? What other things?' There was a hint of genuine confusion in his handsome features, as if he couldn't for one minute imagine there being anything more important than sex. And for him there probably wasn't, she conceded helplessly, flipping the lid of the case shut.

She scraped her hair back from her face and lifted her chin, her eyes challenging as she met his scorching dark gaze. 'Sharing a life, for one thing. Everyday activities. But you wouldn't understand about that because you're well and truly stuck in the Stone Age. For you, a woman's place is flat on her back, preferably stark naked, isn't that right, Luc?' She dropped the bag and spread her hands in a gesture of pure exasperation. 'Do you realise that you've never actually taken me out, Luc? Never. I mean, what exactly was the point of buying me a whole wardrobe full of flashy clothes when I have no need to dress up?'

'Because I like stripping them off you and because I can't see you naked without wanting to be inside you,' he admitted with characteristic frankness and she gave a gurgle of exasperation and fought the temptation to stamp her foot.

'Sex again! Do you realise that once again we haven't actually left this island?'

His dark brows came together in a sharp frown. 'There was no reason to leave. Everything we need is here.'

'Of course it is.' Her voice shook. 'Because all you need when a relationship is based on nothing but sex is a very large bed and maybe not even that if there happens to be a comfortable lift handy.'

His dark eyes narrowed warily. 'You're becoming very emotional—'

'Dead right I'm emotional.' She flung her head back and her hair trailed like tongues of fire down her back. 'I'm a woman and I like being emotional. Believe it or not, I *like* being able to feel things because feeling is what makes us human. You should try it some time; you might find it liberating.'

A muscle flickered in his lean cheek and he gritted his teeth, hanging on to his temper with visible difficulty. 'I can't talk to you when you're like this.'

'You can't talk to me whatever I'm like, Luc.' She dragged the case off the bed and dropped it on the floor. 'You *try* and talk to me but it's such an effort, such an act, that I feel exhausted for you. And you always treat me like a journalist. Giving me sound bites. Things that you're happy for me to hear. Things that sound good. I never get near to the real you.'

'You have been naked underneath the real me for the best part of two weeks,' he reminded her silkily. 'How much nearer could you get?'

Suddenly the fight drained out of her.

He just didn't get it. And he never would. And the sooner she gave up trying to make him understand, the better it would be for both of them.

They were so different it was laughable.

'And those two weeks are now finished,' she reminded him flatly, picking the case up and taking it to the bedroom door. 'You don't know the meaning of the word compromise. There's a flight leaving for London this afternoon. I'd be grateful if you'd ask your pilot to fly me to the airport so that I can catch it. I'm going home to my child. The child you still don't believe exists.'

He stared at her in stunned silence, his expression that of a man trying to comprehend the incomprehensible. Then he muttered something in his own language and turned on his heel, striding out of the room without a backward glance.

Exhausted and drained, Kimberley stared after him, her heart a solid lump of misery in her chest. What had she expected? That he'd argue with her? That he'd make her stay?

That he'd suddenly have a personality transplant and they'd live happily ever after?

She gave herself a mental shake and decided that she was losing her mind.

The two weeks were over and Luc was never, ever going to change. And neither was she. The truth was that the physical attraction between them was so breathtakingly powerful that it blinded her to the truth.

He wasn't what she wanted in a relationship and that was the end of it.

She was never going to share anything other than passion with Luc, and it wasn't enough for her.

She'd done what was needed. Her son was safe. It was time to get on with her life.

Time to go home.

CHAPTER EIGHT

LUNCHTIME came and went with no sign of Luc and Kimberley glanced at her watch with increasing anxiety, afraid that she was going to miss her flight. By mid-afternoon she was sure of it. There was no sign of the helicopter and no sign of Luc.

Short of swimming or flagging down a passing boat, there was no other way off the island.

Feeling hot and tired and furious with Luc for blatantly sabotaging her plans, she was on the point of picking up the phone and seeing whether she could arrange a helicopter taxi to take her to the airport when she finally heard the distinctive sound of a helicopter approaching.

She breathed a sigh of relief. There was no way she'd make it to the airport in time to catch her flight to London, but at least she'd be at the airport ready to take the first available flight the following day.

Keen to leave the island as soon as possible, Kimberley picked up her bag and walked quickly through the lush gardens towards the helicopter pad, wondering whether Luc was even going to bother to say goodbye.

The late afternoon sun was almost unbearably hot and she exchanged a few polite words with the pilot before climbing into the helicopter, eager to protect herself from the heat.

Moments later Luc came striding towards her and he looked so staggeringly handsome that she caught her breath. The casual trousers, swimming trunks, bare torso were gone to be replaced by a designer suit that outlined the male perfection of his body.

There was more to a relationship than the physical, she reminded herself firmly, gritting her teeth and glancing in the opposite direction in an attempt to break the sensual spell his presence cast over her.

He exchanged a few words with one of the bodyguards who was hovering and then joined her in the helicopter, seating himself beside her.

Surely he wasn't coming with her?

She looked at him in surprise, trying not to notice the way his immaculate grey suit showed off the impressive width of his shoulders. He looked every inch the sophisticated, successful tycoon, cool and more than a little remote.

'What are you doing?'

'Exploring the meaning of the word compromise,' he informed her in silky tones, fastening his seat belt in a determined gesture. 'Showing you that I can be as flexible as the next guy when the need arises. If you won't stay here, then I'll come with you.'

She gaped at him.

Luc? Flexible?

He was about as flexible as a steel rod. But, on the other hand, he was sitting next to her, she conceded, feeling slightly weakened by that realisation.

'You're seriously coming with me?' Delight and excitement mingled with sudden panic. Was he coming to see his son? Was he seeking the proof he'd demanded? Or was there another reason? 'Do you have business interests in London?'

'I have business everywhere,' he informed her in a lazy drawl, 'and London is no exception, although perhaps it's only in the last few hours that I developed this burning need to give that particular area of my business my personal attention.'

He leaned forward and issued some instructions to his pilot before relaxing back in his seat.

'Well, I hate to tell you this but we won't be going anywhere today because we've missed the flight,' she informed him and he threw her an amused look.

'The flight leaves when I give orders for it to leave. Not before. We most certainly won't miss it.'

'It takes off in—' she glanced at her watch and pulled a face '—ten minutes, to be precise. And even you can't command a commercial airline.'

'But we're not flying by commercial airline,' he informed her in lazy, almost bored tones as he stretched his long legs out in front of him. 'My private jet is already refuelled and waiting for our arrival.'

His private jet? She blinked at him. 'You have your own plane?'

'Of course.' A dark eyebrow swooped upwards and the amusement in his eyes deepened. 'I have offices all over the world which require my presence on an all too frequent basis. How else did you think I travelled? Flying carpet?'

She blushed and gritted her teeth, feeling ridiculously naïve. 'I've never thought about it at all,' she admitted, 'but I suppose if I had I would have naturally assumed you caught a flight like other people.'

His smile widened. 'But I'm *not* like other people—' he leaned forward, his dark gaze burning into hers '—and two weeks naked in my bed should have convinced you of that fact.'

Vivid, erotic images burst into her brain and she struggled with a ridiculous impulse to slide her arms round his neck.

He was an addiction, she reminded herself firmly, *and no one cured an addiction by continuing to enjoy the addictive substance.*

'Luc—' she cleared her throat and wished he wasn't quite so close to her '—we agreed two weeks and the two weeks is finished.'

'And the next two weeks are just beginning,' he told her helpfully and she looked at him in exasperation.

'Do you know the meaning of the word no?'

He gave a careless shrug of his broad shoulders. 'I'm not that great with "no" or "maybe",' he admitted without a trace of apology, 'but I'm working on "compromise" and "conversation" so who knows?'

She didn't know whether to laugh or hit him. And, no matter how much the rational part of her brain told her that having Luc in London would complicate her life in the extreme, another part lifted and floated with sheer excitement that he'd changed his plans for her. That he was coming to London to be with *her*.

In desperation she tried to stifle that part of herself but failed dismally and spent the entire helicopter flight in a dreamy haze, trying not to read too much into his actions, *trying to drag herself back down from the clouds.* He was still Luc, she reminded herself firmly, and he was never going to change.

At the airport they transferred on to his private jet and Kimberley found it hard to appear cool and indifferent as she was greeted on to the aircraft like royalty.

Once inside, she eyed the luxurious seating area in amazement. 'It's bigger than the average house. And more comfortable, come to that.'

'I do a lot of travelling, so comfort is essential.' He urged her forward into the body of the plane. 'There's a bathroom, a meeting room, a small cinema and an extremely large bedroom.' The sudden gleam in his eyes warned her that they'd be making use of the latter and hot colour touched her cheeks as she gazed around her in amazement.

'Just how rich are you?'

'Shockingly, indecently, *extravagantly* rich,' he assured her calmly, amusement lighting his dark eyes as he registered her ill-disguised awe at this visual demonstration of his wealth, 'which is presumably why you came to me for the five million dollars you needed to pay for your—er—*expenses.*' He waved a hand at the sofa. 'Sit down. We missed lunch and I'm starving and there's an extremely good bottle of Cristal waiting for our attention.'

She sank into the soft embrace of a creamy leather sofa and wondered what it was like to have so much money that you never, ever had to worry again.

They were served by a team of staff who discreetly tended to their every need and then vanished into a different part of the plane, leaving them alone.

'I didn't know you had an office in London.' She sipped her champagne and tucked into spicy chicken served with a delicious side salad.

'I have offices in most of the major cities of the world,' he observed in dry tones, the amusement back in his dark eyes. 'And I didn't know that you had such a burning interest in the detail of my business.'

'That's because we never talk,' she reminded him and he gave her a mocking smile.

'You wish to spend our evenings discussing fourth quarter sales figures?'

She sipped her champagne and realised that she was only just appreciating the true size of his business empire. The truth was that when she was with him she never saw further than the man himself and she'd somehow managed to remain oblivious to the power he yielded. 'And what will you be doing while you're in London?'

One dark eyebrow lifted in abject mockery. 'If you have to ask me that question then I obviously haven't made the objective of my visit clear enough,' he drawled and she felt her heart skitter in her chest.

She shouldn't be flattered. She really shouldn't. *But she was.*

'You're seriously travelling to London to be with me?' She just couldn't contain the little jump in her pulse rate.

'You thought I required a change of scenery?'

Remembering the beauty of his island, she gave a smile. 'Hardly. I just can't quite believe that you changed your plans to be with me.'

Hope flared inside her.

Maybe she'd got him wrong.

Would he cross an ocean just for physical satisfaction? Or was there something more to their relationship, after all?

'The sex between us is truly amazing, *meu amorzinho,*' he replied, 'and in any relationship there must be compromise. You taught me that.'

Hope fizzled out. 'So what you're saying is that you're willing to change countries in order to carry on having sex with me.'

So much for believing that he actually wanted to spend time with her.

'If you're about to pick a fight then I ought to warn you that there is sufficient turbulence outside the plane without causing more on the inside.' He stretched long legs out in front of him, infuriatingly relaxed in the face of her growing tension. 'As you yourself pointed out, I have never before changed my plans for a woman. It's a compliment.'

She bit her lip and refrained from lecturing him on the true definition of the word compliment. It was true that she didn't want to pick a fight. What was the point? He was never going to change and the sooner she accepted that, the happier she'd be.

'Well, we won't be able to spend much time together. I have a business that needs my attention,' she said flatly. And a son. *A son who Luc still didn't believe existed.* 'Unlike you, I don't have a massive staff willing to do the work in my absence. Having been away for two weeks, I have lots of catching up to do.'

'My hotel suite comes complete with my own staff and full office facilities, which you are welcome to use,' he offered smoothly and she felt herself tense.

'I don't need office space,' she said quickly. 'I've been away for two weeks, Luc. There are people I need to see.'

There was a sardonic gleam in his dark eyes as he studied her. 'But presumably your evenings and nights will be available.'

She should say no. She should tell him that their relationship was over. 'Possibly.' She put down her fork, leaving her food untouched. Being with Luc unsettled her stomach so much that she couldn't face food. 'I'll meet you for dinner.'

Once Rio was tucked up in bed and asleep.

What was wrong with that? she asked herself weakly. She was already crazily in love with Luc. What did she have to lose by spending more time with him?

They landed in the early morning in time to get stuck in the commuter traffic that crawled its way into London on a daily basis during the week and Luc had plenty of opportunity to contemplate the distinct possibility that he'd suffered a personality change.

Never in his life before had he suffered an impulse to adjust his plans for a woman, least of all follow one halfway across the world. The fact that he was now in London, a city that hadn't featured as part of his immediate plans, left him suffering from no small degree of discomfort.

And if he needed any confirmation of the fact that he

was acting out of character, then he simply had to look at Kimberley's face.

It was hard to say who was more shocked, he mused with wry amusement as he cast a sideways look at the woman who had wrought this miraculous change in him. She was clearly wondering what on earth was going on and he could hardly blame her. He was still telling himself that it was just about great sex and certainly the night they'd spent on his plane had given him plenty of evidence to support that assumption. The fact that he'd never gone to similar lengths for any woman before was something he preferred not to dwell on.

'I haven't even asked you where you live.'

The way she looked at him reminded him of a small vulnerable animal trapped in the headlights of an oncoming car. 'I bought a small flat with your money,' she reminded him calmly. 'If you just drop me at your office I'll make my own way home and meet you at your hotel later.'

Luc watched her intently. *Was she planning to meet her lover?*

'Fine.' He agreed to her terms, taking the way she immediately relaxed as confirmation of his suspicions.

She'd assured him that she didn't have a man in her life, but the evidence appeared to suggest otherwise, he thought grimly.

It started to rain heavily as they approached the London office of Santoro Investments, which was situated in Canary Wharf along with many of the other leading merchant banks.

'My driver will take you home,' he informed her smoothly, leaning across to give her a lingering kiss on the mouth. 'I'll order dinner for eight.'

After which he intended to drive all thoughts of other men clean out of her mind.

His relationship with women was the one area of his life

where he'd never before encountered competition but he was entirely confident that he was more than up to the task.

Having issued a set of instructions to his driver in his native language, Luc stepped out of the car and contemplated the degree of havoc he was about to cause in an office unprepared for his imminent arrival.

Flanked by members of his security team, who had been in the car behind, he strode towards the building, trying to recall exactly how he'd intended to justify his unexpected visit to his London office to his amazed staff.

Kimberley spent the day catching up on some urgent business issues, talking to Jason and watching the clock, anxious for the moment when she could pick her son up from school.

When his little figure finally appeared at the school gates she was struck by his powerful resemblance to his father. He had the same night-black hair and the same dark eyes. Perhaps it was because she'd just spent two weeks with Luc that the similarity was so marked, she thought as she swept him into her arms and cuddled him close. *She'd missed him so much.*

They chatted non-stop all the way home to the tiny flat she shared with Jason and carried on chatting while she made tea.

Kimberley had just cleared Rio's plate when the doorbell rang.

'I'll get it.' Jason stood up and gave her a smile. 'You two still have a lot to talk about.'

He strolled out of the room to answer the door but was back only moments later, this time without the smile.

'Who was—?' Kimberley broke off as she caught sight of the tall, powerfully built figure standing beside him. Her heart dropped like a stone.

'Luc.' She stood up quickly, her chair scraping on the tiled floor of the kitchen, her knees shaking and the breath suddenly trapped in her lungs. *What was he doing here?* 'I was going to come to you at eight.'

'I finished in the office early and decided to surprise you.' There was an edge to his voice that alerted her to danger and she lifted a hand to her throat.

'But you didn't know my address—'

He gave a cool smile. 'You were careful to keep it a secret. I wanted to know why.' His eyes slid to Jason and then he noticed the child. A slight frown touched his dark brows and then his expression shifted swiftly from cool to shattered.

'*Meu Deus*, it can't be—' His voice was hoarse and his handsome face was suddenly alarmingly pale under his tan. He looked totally shell-shocked.

Kimberley suddenly found she couldn't move. She made a nervous gesture with her hand. 'I *did* tell you—'

His gaze fixed on her, his dark eyes fierce and hot and loaded with accusation. 'But you *knew* I didn't believe you—'

She stared at him helplessly. 'We should go outside to talk about this—'

For a long moment he didn't respond. Appeared to have lost his ability to speak. Then, finally, he found his voice.

'Why?' He didn't shift his gaze from the child. 'If this is really how it appears, then *why* am I discovering this now? *After seven years!*'

Kimberley held her breath, trapped by the anger and emotional tension that throbbed in his powerful frame. She was on the verge of sweeping Rio into her arms, afraid that he'd pick up the same vibes as her, afraid that he'd be upset. But, far from being upset, he was staring at his father in blatant fascination.

'You look like me.'

Luc inhaled sharply and his proud head jerked backwards as if he'd been slapped. 'Yes.'

Kimberley closed her eyes and asked herself why her child couldn't have been born with red hair. As it was, the resemblance between father and son was so striking that there could be absolutely no doubt about the boy's parentage.

She felt Luc's tension build. Felt his anger, his uncertainty, *his agony*, and guilt sliced through her like the blade of the sharpest knife.

For the first time since she'd known him, all his emotions were clearly etched on every plane of his handsome face for all to read, and the vision of such a private man revealing himself so completely deepened her guilt still further.

She held her breath, not knowing how to rescue the situation, just praying that he wouldn't say anything that would upset their child.

He didn't.

Instead he hunkered down so that his eyes were on the same level as the boy's. 'I'm Luc.'

Her son's eyes fixed on his father for the first time in his life. 'You look cross. Are you cross?'

'Not cross,' Luc assured him, his voice decidedly unsteady and his smile a little shaky. 'I just wasn't expecting to meet you, that's all.'

'I'm Rio.'

Luc closed his eyes briefly and the breath hissed through his teeth. 'It isn't a very common name.'

'I'm named after a very special city,' Rio confided happily, sliding off his chair and walking over to a wall of the kitchen which was covered in his paintings, photos and cards. 'This is it.' He tugged a card from the wall and handed it to Luc with a smile. 'That's where I get my name. That's the mountain Corcovado with the statue *Cristo Redento*—' he pronounced it perfectly '—doesn't it look great? I'm going to go there one day. Mum's promised. But it's a long way away and we don't have enough money yet. We're saving up.'

There was a long painful silence as Luc stared down at the postcard in his hand and then he lifted his gaze and looked straight at Kimberley, raw accusation shimmering in his dark eyes.

She stood totally still, unable to move, paralysed by the terrifying anger she sensed building inside him. But this was like no anger she'd ever encountered before. This wasn't a raw red anger, quick to ignite into flames of vicious temper. This was a blue cold anger, a simmering menace that threatened a far more lethal outcome.

Her courage shifted and, for no immediate reason that she could identify, she felt afraid. 'Luc—'

'Not now and not in front of the child,' he growled before dragging a deep breath into his lungs and turning his attention back to Rio.

Kimberley watched in a state of breathless tension, marvelling at the change in him, at how much he softened his attitude when he looked at their son. The anger seemed to drain away to be replaced by a gentle fascination. 'It's a lovely picture. A great city.' His voice was soft and he smoothed a bronzed hand over Rio's dark curls in a surprisingly tender gesture. 'Those paintings on the wall—did you do them?'

'I'm going to be an artist,' Rio confided, slipping his hand into Luc's and dragging him towards the wall where the paintings were proudly displayed. 'That's my favourite.' He pointed to one in particular and Luc nodded.

'I can see why. It's very good.' His expression was serious as he studied every childish brushstroke with enormous interest.

Kimberley felt her heart twist with guilt.

She'd made the wrong decision.

She'd robbed him of the right to know his son. And her son of the right to know his father. Suddenly she could hardly breathe. But what else could she have done? she reasoned.

She'd *tried* to tell him. She'd wanted, *needed*, his support right at the beginning. But he'd made it clear that the relationship was over. And she'd seen a man like her father.

'You can have it if you like,' Rio offered generously and there was a long silence while Luc continued to stare at the painting. Then he swallowed hard and cleared his throat.

'Thanks.' He glanced down at his son and the roughness of his tone betrayed his emotion. 'I'd like that.'

He carefully removed the painting from the wall and held it as if it were priceless. Then he crouched down again and started to talk to his son. He asked questions, he listened, he responded and all the time Kimberley watched, transfixed by what she was seeing.

How could he be so good with children?

He had absolutely no experience with children. He should have been at a loss and yet here he was, totally comfortable, talking to a six-year-old boy about football, painting and any other subject that Rio chose to bring up.

Eventually he glanced at his Rolex and brought the conversation to a reluctant halt. 'Unfortunately, I have to go now.'

Rio frowned. 'Will I see you again?'

'Oh, yes.' Luc's voice was still gentle but his broad shoulders were rigid with simmering tension. 'You'll definitely see me again. Very soon.'

Kimberley's heart kicked hard against her chest as she was forced to face the inevitable. 'Luc—'

Finally he looked at her, his gaze hard and uncompromising. 'Eight o'clock.' His tone was icy cold. 'I'll send my driver for you. We'll talk then. I think you might find it's a skill I've finally mastered.'

CHAPTER NINE

KIMBERLEY paused outside the door to Luc's suite and took a moment to compose herself.

Was he still as angry as he'd been when he'd left the house?

She took a deep breath and felt dread seep through her like a heavy substance, weighing her down. Whichever way you looked at it, this wasn't going to be an easy meeting.

And she didn't feel at all prepared. For the past seven years she'd convinced herself that even if she *had* managed to get close enough to Luc to tell him about her pregnancy then he would have completely rejected the prospect of fatherhood. This was a man who couldn't sustain a relationship for longer than a month, whose lifestyle was so far removed from that of a family man that it was laughable. There had been nothing about him to suggest that hearing the word 'pregnancy' would have stimulated a reaction other than panic and after he'd flatly refused to see her she'd managed to convince herself that it was all for the best.

But today, seeing him interacting with his son, she'd asked herself the same question she'd been asking herself for the past seven years. *Had she done the wrong thing by not persisting in her attempts to contact Luc and tell him the truth?*

Certainly Luc had appeared far from horrified by the realisation that he actually did have a son. Shocked, yes. Angry with her, yes. But horrified? No. In fact, his reaction had been so far from what she'd predicted all those years ago that it merely confirmed, yet again, how little she knew him. *He'd surprised her.*

And now he was expecting an explanation.

She was shown into the enormous living room of the suite by one of the security guards, who immediately melted into the background, leaving her alone with Luc. He was standing with his back to the window, facing into the room.

Waiting for her.

He watched her in silence, his handsome face cold and unsmiling, his long legs planted firmly apart in an attitude of pure male aggression.

The silence dragged on and on and in the end she was the one to break it, unable to bear the rising tension a moment longer.

She curled her fingers into her palms. 'Luc—'

'I don't even want to talk about this until we have resolved the issue of the blackmailer. Evidently someone really is threatening my child. I want that letter and I want it now.' He held out his hand and she delved in her handbag and produced it.

'There are absolutely no clues as to who sent it, he—'

'It isn't your job to look for clues.' Luc spoke into his mobile phone and moments later a man who Kimberley recognised as his head of security walked into the room.

He spoke briefly to Luc, took the letter and then walked out of the room, pausing only to give a reassuring smile to Kimberley, who stared after him in surprise.

'Doesn't he want to ask me anything?'

Luc gave a cool smile. 'I don't micromanage my staff. I appoint people based on their skills to do the job and then I leave the job up to them. Ronaldo is the best there is. If he feels the need to question you then doubtless he'll do so. In the meantime I have arranged for Rio to have twenty-four hour security both inside and outside the home.'

She gaped at him and her stomach curled with fear. 'You think he's still in danger?'

'He's my son,' Luc pointed out coldly, 'and that alone is enough to put him in danger. He'll be under guard here until I can arrange to take him back to Brazil.'

The room spun. 'You're *not* taking my child to Brazil! I know you're angry about all this, but—'

'*Our child*, Kimberley. We are talking about *our* child and angry doesn't even *begin* to describe what I am feeling at this precise moment,' he informed her in dangerously soft tones, every muscle in his powerful body pumped up and tense as he struggled for control. 'I am waiting for an explanation and I don't even know why, because frankly there *is* no explanation sufficient to justify your failure to inform me that I have been a father for the past six years.'

'I told you two weeks ago—'

'Because you needed my help! If it hadn't been for the blackmail letter the chances are I *never* would have found out, isn't that right?' He paced the floor of the hotel suite, his anger and volatility barely contained. 'I can't believe you would have kept my son from me!' His eyes flashed bitter condemnation and she stiffened defensively, his total lack of self-recrimination firing her own anger.

The fact that he hadn't even considered his own behaviour in the whole situation filled her with outrage.

He was laying the blame squarely on her and yet she knew that had he agreed to see her when she'd tried to contact him she would have told him immediately.

'I don't have to justify anything, Luc.' Her voice shook but she carried on anyway, determined not to let him bully her. 'You treated me abominably.'

'And this was my punishment?' He stared at her in derision. 'Because I ended our relationship, you decided that I'd forfeited the right to know about my child?'

'No.' Her own temper exploded in the face of his accusing look. 'But you're supposed to take responsibility for your actions. You were eager enough to sleep with me but considerably less eager to find out whether I was pregnant, weren't you, Luc?'

The faintest flicker of a frown touched those strong dark brows. 'I did *not* ignore the possibility,' he gritted, 'but I used protection. There was no reason for you to become pregnant.'

'And that's it? Your responsibility ends there? Well, I'm sorry to be the one to point out that you're not infallible,' she said bitterly, 'and your so-called "protection" didn't work. I discovered I was pregnant the day after I left your house.'

'You were still in Rio de Janeiro when you discovered your pregnancy?' His gaze changed from startled to scornful and he swept a hand through the air in a gesture of disgust. 'Then it would have taken *nothing* for you to come and find me and tell me.'

His condemnation was the final straw. 'You have a selective memory. It's so easy for you to stand there now and say that, but at the time you wouldn't let me come *near* you!' Her body trembled with outrage and her hair tumbled over her shoulders, emphasising the pallor of her face. 'You'd had enough of me, Luc. Remember? You went out partying, just to prove that you were bored with me. And when I did the same you lost your temper. We hardly parted on good terms.'

His gaze was ice-cold. 'This wasn't about us. It was about a child. You had a responsibility to tell me.'

'How?' She almost choked on the word. 'How was I supposed to tell you? Do you realise how *impossible* it is to get near to you unless you give permission? It's easier to see royalty than get an audience with you!'

He frowned. 'You're being ridiculous—'

'Not ridiculous, Luc.' She smoothed her hair away from her face and forced herself to calm down. 'You are totally in-

accessible to the public and you should know that because you made yourself that way.'

'But you were not the public.' His gaze raked her face with raw anger. 'We had a relationship.'

'But once that relationship was over I had no better access to you than anyone else. I couldn't get through the walls of bodyguards and frosty-faced receptionists to exchange a single word with you.'

'You obviously didn't try hard enough.'

The injustice of the suggestion stung like acid in an open wound. 'Cast your mind back, Luc.' She wrapped her arms around her waist to stop the shivering. It was a warm June evening but suddenly she felt cold. 'Twice I rang asking to see you and twice you refused to take my call. You thought I'd left Brazil and then suddenly, two weeks after our relationship had ended, I made a final attempt to tell you I was pregnant. This time I turned up in your office asking to see you. I thought that if I came myself then it would be harder to send me away. Your response was to arrange for your driver to take me to the airport, just to make sure that this time there could be no doubt that I'd left the country. It was what you wanted, Luc, so it was what I did.'

He stiffened but had the grace to look uncomfortable. 'I assumed you wanted to talk about our relationship.'

'No. I wanted to tell you I was *pregnant*. But you wouldn't listen. So I went home and did everything by myself. You thought I was a gold digger— ' Shaking with anger and the sheer injustice of it all, she dug a hand into her bag and pulled out a sheaf of papers. 'Here are the receipts, Luc. Everything I spent is itemised there, down to the last box of nappies, and there isn't a single pair of shoes on the list. Just for the record, I *hated* having to use your money and I only did it for Rio.'

She stuffed the papers into his hand and had the satisfaction of seeing him speechless.

He stared at the papers for a moment, his handsome face unusually pale. 'I did *not* know you were pregnant.'

'You didn't give me a chance to tell you! You'd already made up your mind that our relationship was over.' She felt tears clog her throat. 'And it *was* over. Maybe it's a good thing I didn't manage to tell you the truth. What would have happened? You'd never stayed with a woman for more than a month, Luc.'

He threw the papers on to the nearest sofa and paced the length of the suite until he ran out of room. Then he turned to face her, his eyes glittering dark and fierce. 'I would *not* have abandoned a child—'

'But the child would have come with a mother,' she reminded him flatly. 'Complicated, isn't it? Would you have abandoned your playboy lifestyle to give your son a home?'

He jabbed long fingers through his sleek dark hair, clearly driven to the edges of his patience. 'I do not know what I would have done—but finding out this way, it is very difficult—'

Goaded past the point of noticing that his usually fluent English was less than perfect, she turned on him. '*You're* finding it difficult? Try discovering you're pregnant at the age of eighteen when you're unemployed and on your own in a foreign city. I was totally alone, scared, jobless and homeless. *That's* difficult, Luc!'

His broad shoulders tensed. 'You must have had family who could help you—'

'Well, I didn't exactly meet their parental expectations.' She tried to hide the hurt because the truth was that she still couldn't quite believe that her parents had both turned away her pleas for help. She couldn't imagine any situation where she would refuse to help her son. 'They didn't approve of my modelling career but they approved even less of my career as your mistress and the fact that I'd abandoned *everything* to be with you.'

From the moment she'd laid eyes on him she'd been dazzled. Everything else in her life had become inconsequential. *Nothing* had mattered except Luc.

His eyes meshed with hers and she could see that he too was remembering the sensual madness of the time they'd spent together.

Disapproval emanated from every inch of his powerful frame. 'They should have supported you—'

'Perhaps. But you don't always get what you deserve in life and people don't always behave the way they should.' She shot him a meaningful look and had the satisfaction of seeing two spots of colour appear high on his cheekbones. 'The only support I had were your two credit cards, so don't talk to me about difficult, Luc, because I've been there and done that. And don't keep telling me that I did the wrong thing. I tried to tell you. Yes, I failed, but some of the responsibility for that failure lies with you, so don't give me that self-righteous, I'm-so-perfect look! Maybe you should rethink the way you run your life. Ex-girlfriends who think they might be pregnant should be given priority when your staff are handing out appointments to see you.' She picked up her bag and walked towards the door, suddenly feeling a desperate need for fresh air and space. The past was closing in on her and she had to get away.

His voice stopped her. 'You're *not* walking out of here.'

'Watch me!' She turned to look at him, her hair tumbling past her shoulders, her gaze challenging him to stop her if he dared. 'This conversation is clearly going nowhere and I'm tired.'

'Then we will continue the conversation sitting down.' He gestured towards the nearest sofa. 'We have much to discuss still.'

'But we're not discussing,' she pointed out tightly, 'we're arguing, and I've had enough for one night. I've had enough of your accusations and your total inability to see the situation from anyone's point of view but your own. So I'm going home. And when you've calmed down enough to think properly, then maybe we'll talk.'

His hard jaw clenched. 'I have arranged dinner.'

'I'd rather starve than eat dinner with you.' Driven by hurt and frustration, she yanked the door open, ignoring the startled gaze of the bodyguard stationed outside the door. 'And if you've got an appetite at this particular moment in time, then you're even more insensitive than I thought.'

After a sleepless night spent reliving every moment of their conversation, Kimberley was drinking strong coffee at the kitchen table when the doorbell rang.

It was Luc and judging from the shadows under his eyes and the growth of stubble on his hard jaw, his night hadn't been any better than hers.

But he still managed to look devastating, she thought helplessly, running her eyes over his broad shoulders.

His eyes were wary, as if he wasn't sure what reaction to expect. 'Can I come in?'

'What for?' She lifted her chin. 'More recriminations, Luc? More blame?'

A muscle flickered in his hard jaw. 'No recriminations or blame. But you have to admit that we do have things to talk about.'

'I'm not sure that we do.'

His eyes flashed, dark and angry. '*Meu Deus*, I am doing my best here but you won't even meet me halfway!'

'It isn't you or I that matter in this, Luc! It's Rio. I won't have him upset. And I don't trust your temper.'

'There is nothing wrong with my temper!' Luc inhaled deeply and dragged long fingers through his hair, visibly struggling for control. 'I admit that I was angry last night but I'm over that now and I would never upset Rio. Did he look upset yesterday, when he met me?' His voice was a masculine growl. 'Did he?'

She forced herself to stand her ground. 'No. But he didn't know who you were. It isn't just about your temper, Luc, although you definitely need to work on that. You're about to upset his life and I won't let you do it.'

Luc's jaw clenched. 'I have no intention of upsetting anyone.'

'No?' Her tone was cold. 'The way you didn't upset me last night?'

A muscle flickered in his jaw. 'I may have been slightly unfair to you—' he conceded finally and she fought a powerful temptation to slap his handsome face.

'Slightly?'

He shrugged broad shoulders and looked distinctly uncomfortable. 'All right, very possibly more than slightly—' his accent was more pronounced than usual '—but that is all in the past now and we have to talk about the future.'

'That's it?' Kimberley gave an incredulous laugh. 'That's your idea of an apology? Push it into the past and forget about it? How very convenient.'

He swore under his breath. 'It is true that there are many things I regret about what has happened but the past is history and the most important thing is that we concentrate on the future.'

'That's it?' Kimberley shook her head in weary disbelief. 'You need to add "apology" to your list of things you're going to work on, along with "no", "compromise" and "conversation".'

'*Meu Deus, what* do you expect me to do?' He displayed all the explosive volatility of a man well and truly wedged in a tight corner. 'I can't change what happened but I *can* make it right now. But we need to talk.'

'We said everything that needed to be said last night,' Kimberley said stiffly and he gave a driven sigh.

'We were both in a state of shock last night and we have both had time to do some thinking,' he muttered, glancing over his shoulder to where his car and driver waited. 'This is all new territory for me and I certainly don't want to explore it in public. Are you going to let me come in or are we going to provide headlines for tomorrow's newspapers?'

What was the point of refusing? She'd known when she'd walked away from him the night before that she was only postponing the inevitable.

She opened the door a little wider and he strode past her and made straight for her kitchen.

'This is a nice room—' His eyes drifted to the French windows that opened on to the tiny garden. 'It has a nice atmosphere. You chose well.'

Given that her entire flat would have fitted into one room of the villa, she took his words as a sign that he was at least attempting to be conciliatory.

'Thanks.'

He tilted his head and scanned the four corners of the room. 'Its value must have increased considerably since you purchased it.'

She stared at him with undisguised incredulity. 'Do you only ever think about money and return on investment?'

'No, sometimes I think about sex and now I also have a child to think about.' His eyes were cool as he glanced around him. 'Has Jason lived with you from the start? It was Jason you were talking to on the phone?'

'Yes.' She made a pot of coffee. 'He was the only friend I had.'

'It's good that I'm aware that Jason's sexual preferences don't run to beautiful female models,' Luc drawled and something in his tone made her glance at him warily.

'Why's that?'

'Because it saves me having to knock his teeth down his

throat,' he said pleasantly, the gleam in his dark eyes making her catch her breath.

'You and I were no longer an item, Luc,' she pointed out, pouring them both a coffee and taking the mugs to the table, 'so jealousy on your part is nothing short of ridiculous. I could have been with any number of men quite legitimately.'

The atmosphere in the room instantly darkened.

'And were you?' His voice was a threatening male growl and she gave an impatient sigh.

'No, Luc, I wasn't. I had a baby, I was struggling to build a business and I was always exhausted. The last thing I needed was the additional mental strain of a man. And, frankly, my experience with you was enough to put me off men for life.'

'Not exactly for life,' he said softly, lifting his mug to his lips and sipping his coffee. 'I seem to recall you displaying no small degree of enthusiasm over the past two weeks. Not exactly the reaction of a woman who has gone off men.'

Her eyes met his and she swallowed hard. 'That's different.'

'*Not* different.' He looked at her thoughtfully, his gaze curiously intent. 'Perhaps what you're saying, *meu amorzinho*, is that you failed to find another man who made you feel the way I did. Perhaps what you're saying is that being with me put you off other men for life because none of them matched up.'

Her jaw dropped at his arrogance even while a tiny voice in her head told her that he was absolutely right. No man had ever come close to making her feel what she felt for Luc and she doubted that any man ever would. 'Your ego is amazing—'

'I'm merely telling the truth.' He was cool, confident and totally back in control. It was as if that split second moment of regret and apology had never happened. 'It is time to be totally honest with each other. It's essential if our marriage is to work.'

If she'd been holding her coffee she would have dropped it. 'Our marriage?' She almost choked on the word. 'What marriage?'

'It's the obvious way forward.' He gave a dismissive shrug as if marriage had frequently featured in his plans in the past. 'We share a child. It makes sense for us to share the other aspects of our lives as well.'

She gaped at him and struggled to find her voice. 'We share nothing.'

He gave a smug male smile. 'I think the last two weeks have proved that isn't true.'

'You're talking about sex again, Luc!' Kimberley rose to her feet, resisting the temptation to scream with frustration. She couldn't believe what she was hearing. 'You cannot possibly base a marriage on what we have!'

His smile faded. 'We have a son,' he said coldly, 'and that's more than enough of a basis for a marriage.'

She flopped back down on to her chair. 'You're delusional,' she said flatly and he stared at her with naked incredulity.

'Is that any way to respond to a proposal of marriage?'

'Possibly not, but you didn't make a proposal of marriage,' she said bitterly, standing up again and pacing round her tiny kitchen in an attempt to work off some of her anger and frustration. 'You marched in here and announced that we're getting married because we have a child.'

Jaw clenched, he stood up too. 'I have never proposed to a woman before—'

'Then trust me, you need more practice.' She lifted an eyebrow in his direction. 'Perhaps by the fourth or fifth attempt you might get it right.'

He reached out and grabbed her, his lean strong fingers gripping her arms as he forced her to look at him. 'Stop pacing and listen to me. I mean that you should be flattered. Do you know how many women have wanted to hear me say those words?'

'What words exactly?' She stared at him in helpless frustration. '"*We share a child. It makes sense for us to share the other aspects of our lives as well"*? That certainly wasn't in any of the fairy tales I read as a child.'

'*Stop* making a joke—'

'Do I look as though I'm laughing?' She tried to wriggle away from him but he held her firmly. 'Believe me, Luc, I've never been as far away from laughing. You've just insulted me beyond belief.'

'*Meu Deus*, how have I insulted you?' He stared down at her with ill-concealed exasperation. 'I am asking you to marry me.'

She tilted her head to one side, significantly unimpressed. 'And why would I want to do that? Because it's an honour bestowed on so few?'

'Because it is the best thing for our child,' he growled with a dangerous flash of his dark eyes. 'And because it's what women always want from men.'

And the stupid thing was it was exactly what she wanted. *But not like this.*

'You think so?' Her tone dripped sarcasm. 'Well, not this woman, Luc. I can't think of anything worse than tying myself to you.'

'You are not thinking straight.'

'I'm thinking perfectly straight. Marriage to you would be a nightmare. I'd never be able to go out because you're so hideously possessive, we wouldn't have any sort of social life because your idea of an evening with me is to be naked in bed. You probably wouldn't allow me to get dressed!'

He inhaled sharply, his face unusually pale under his tan. 'You're becoming very emotional.'

'Too right I'm emotional! *"We share a child. It makes sense for us to share the other aspects of our lives as well."* What about the things that matter, Luc, like love and affection? I grew up with a man like you. My father felt the need to go to bed with every woman who smiled at him! Our house was filled with "aunties" and, believe me, there is absolutely no way I'd inflict a similar childhood on a child of mine.'

'That is *not* the way I would behave.' His hand sliced through the air in a gesture of outrage. 'It's true that there is no love between us but marriage can be successful based on other things.'

'Like what? Sex?' She threw him a derisory look. 'For a marriage to work a couple at least have to be able to spend time in each other's company, preferably dressed. That's the bare minimum, Luc, especially when there's a child involved.'

Luc studied her thoughtfully. 'So if we spend time together, then you'll say yes? Those are your terms?'

Terms?

'You make it sound like another of your business negotiations.'

He gave a slight shrug. 'And in a way it is. We each have something that the other wants.'

'You have nothing that I want.'

He leaned back in his chair, his eyes holding hers. 'You want Rio to grow up not knowing his father?'

She bit her lip and shifted slightly. 'No, but—'

'So if we can find a way of sharing an existence amicably then it would be what you would want for him?'

'Well, yes, but—'

'Name your terms.'

She stared at him in stupefied silence. *Name your terms?* Was he that desperate to get his hands on Rio?

'It isn't that simple. I—'

'It is exactly that simple.' As usual he was arrogantly confident of his ability to manoeuvre the situation to his advantage. 'Tell me what it is you want and I will give it to you.'

Love. She wanted him to love her.

She bit back a hysterical laugh, imagining Luc's reaction

if she were to deliver that as her ultimatum. He thought that he could deliver anything she asked, but of course he couldn't. And she would be asking the impossible.

'So I tell you what I want, you say yes and then we get married.'

'That's right.' He gave a confident smile, evidently relieved that she'd finally understood.

'And then you revert to your old ways.'

He frowned. 'I want this marriage to work—'

'But you've never exactly excelled at commitment before, have you, Luc? What's your longest relationship up until now? A month? Two months?'

'There has never been a child involved before—'

'Maybe not, but two months to a lifetime is still rather a stretch,' she muttered, 'and I think it might tax your staying power.'

'I will do whatever it takes to make it work.'

'Really?' She looked at him curiously. 'You'll do whatever it takes?'

'Whatever it takes.'

What did she have to lose?

'All right, this is what it's going to take.' She folded her arms and tilted her head to one side. 'For the next month all our meetings will take place fully clothed. You're going to take me out and you're going to take Rio out. We're going to behave like a family, Luc. And every evening you're going to have me home by ten o'clock. No overnight stays and no sex. And no sex with anyone else, either. If I see one incriminating photograph of you in the press, the deal is off.'

The air throbbed with sudden tension. 'No sex?'

It was hard not to laugh at his tone of utter disbelief.

'No sex. I'm sure you'll be able to hold yourself back for the greater good of proving that being a good father to your child is what really matters to you. And it will give us a chance to find out whether we can stand being together when there is no sex involved. If we can—' she shrugged her slender shoulders '—then I'll marry you.'

She smiled placidly, safe in the knowledge that he was about to leap to his feet and reject her terms as totally unreasonable.

He was a red-blooded highly sexed male in his prime. He was *never* going to agree to her terms.

And that was fine by her. She didn't want to marry Luc. He didn't love her and he never would, and spending every day with him, knowing that he was only with her because of their child, would be torment.

'All right.'

She was so busy smiling to herself that at first she thought she'd misheard him. 'Sorry?'

'I said all right.' He rose to his feet and walked towards her, a slightly dangerous glint in his dark, sexy eyes. 'I accept your terms.'

She looked at him dubiously. 'All of them?'

'All of them.'

'You do?' She stared at him in confusion and a slight smile touched his hard mouth.

'I do. And pretty soon I'll be saying those words in a marriage ceremony, *meu amorzinho*, because you are going to enjoy spending time with me, and so is Rio.'

Kimberley gaped at him. Did anything dent his confidence?

He'd never manage it, she told herself firmly.

Deprived of sex and forced to communicate on a daily basis would soon put an end to his desire for marriage, she thought wryly, and then perhaps her life could return to normal. Obviously Luc would need access to his son, but that could be easily arranged.

'Fine,' she said airily. 'It's a deal.'

* * *

Luc strode away from the house, wondering at exactly what point he'd lost his sanity.

He'd just agreed to a month without sex with a woman who made him think about nothing but sex.

What sort of normal healthy guy would agree to terms like that?

Had he gone totally and utterly mad?

For a man who'd made a point of avoiding commitment at all costs, he was more than a little disturbed by how far he was prepared to go to persuade Kimberley to marry him.

And she *would* marry him, of course, because he would meet all her terms.

How hard could it be? Conversation? Easy—he was getting better at it by the day. Family trips out—easy. No sex—not so easy, he conceded ruefully, ignoring the waiting car and striding purposefully in the opposite direction. But perhaps if she was fully clothed the whole time they were together and he took lots of cold showers, he might just be able to manage it.

Which meant that the deal was as good as done.

One month, that was all it was, he reminded himself as he crossed the road without noticing the cars.

And then he could be a proper father to his son.

Because that was what this marriage was all about.

What other possible reason could there be?

CHAPTER TEN

ONE month later Kimberley sat in the pretty, airy sitting room of her flat, wondering what had happened to her life.

The room was filled with the scent of yet more fresh flowers, which had arrived from Luc that morning, and around her neck lay a beautiful necklace, which he'd given her only the night before as they'd shared another intimate dinner on her patio.

If she'd thought he wasn't capable of sustaining a relationship outside the bedroom then she'd been proved more than wrong.

She stared down at her sketch-book, which lay in front of her, open and untouched. She'd promised herself that today she was going to do some rough designs of a necklace for a very wealthy French client, but so far she hadn't as much as glanced at the page in front of her. She was too distracted.

She couldn't stop thinking about Luc.

It was ironic, she mused as she gazed out of the window without so much as a glance at the sketch-pad in front of her, that the first time she and Luc had spent time together fully clothed and without a double bed in sight had been on a visit to London Zoo with their son.

And the ridiculous thing was that *they'd felt like a family.* It didn't matter how many times she reminded herself that he didn't love her and that this amazing, romantic month was all about him trying to manipulate her into marrying him so that he could have full access to his son, she still couldn't stop feeling ridiculously happy.

The almost agonizing anxiety she'd felt over the kidnap threat had finally vanished, partly because she'd heard nothing more from the man and partly because Luc's security team were now part of her everyday life.

But the real reason for her happiness was that she just adored being with Luc. And today she was missing him. That morning he'd been forced to fly to Paris for an urgent business meeting and already she was watching the clock, anticipating the time when his flight would land.

She'd been fast discovering that as well as being amazing in bed, Luc was also incredibly entertaining company when he wanted to be and she was enjoying seeing a completely different side of him.

From the moment he had announced his intention of marrying her, his entire focus had been on her and Rio. He'd contacted lawyers, changed his will, signed countless documents and presented her with countless documents to sign, all designed to ensure that Rio was well provided for. And he'd spent endless hours with his son, waiting at the school gates to collect him at the end of the school day and then taking him on trips, giving him treats and just *talking*.

With the insensitivity of youth, Rio was always asking him questions and Luc had started to relax and respond, gradually becoming more open about himself and his past. And that willingness to reveal intimate details about himself had extended into the evenings, when Rio was safely tucked up in his bed. London was experiencing a heatwave and Luc and Kimberley had fallen into a habit of eating dinner in the tiny walled garden that led from her kitchen and the intimacy of their surroundings had somehow stimulated conversations of a deeply personal nature.

In the past few days alone she'd learned that both his parents had died when he was thirteen and that he'd been given a home by Maria, the woman who was now his personal assistant. And in return he'd given her a job. And she'd been with him for over twenty years.

Maybe Luc *was* capable of commitment, Kimberley mused as she picked up her pencil and attempted to translate the design in her head into a drawing that would provide the basis of her first discussion with her client. After all, he was obviously committed to Maria. And he was showing all the signs of being equally committed to his son.

Committed enough to make an effort in his relationship with her.

She was far too realistic to pretend, even for one unguarded minute, that all this effort on his part was driven by anything other than a desire to secure unlimited access to their child.

With her agreement, he'd revealed his identity to Rio immediately and if she'd harboured any doubts about the sense of marrying a man who clearly didn't love her, then they had dissolved once she'd seen the undiluted excitement and delight on her child's face when he'd finally realised that this vibrant, energetic, exotic man was his father.

How could she deprive her child of the chance to grow up in a normal family? Particularly as Luc himself was so clearly determined to be the very best father possible.

And he'd met every one of her terms. All too easily, it would seem.

Was she the only one who was sexually frustrated? she wondered ruefully.

Evidently the answer was yes. Luc hadn't made one single move in her direction in the past month. He kissed her on both cheeks when they met and when they parted and that was the limit of their physical contact. Very formal. Very restrained.

The desperate need to touch him and be touched by him was driving her mad.

And they were getting on well, she conceded as her pencil danced over the page, creating a stunning individual design. She enjoyed the time they spent together. Enjoyed spending time with him, even though she knew he was doing it with a distinct purpose in mind.

All right, so their relationship wasn't perfect, but what relationship was? She'd learned at eighteen that fairy tale endings didn't happen in real life and at least she was with Luc and Rio had a father. The fact that Luc didn't love her had almost ceased to matter.

As long as she was careful not to reveal the strength of her feelings, careful to do nothing which might frighten him off, what could go wrong?

Kimberley glanced at the clock again. She'd arranged to pick Rio up from school half an hour early so that they could go and meet Luc at the airport. Wasn't that what families did?

The phone rang and, expecting Luc's call, she lifted the receiver and tucked it under her ear, leaving her hands free to gather up her sketches.

But it wasn't Luc and her face turned pale as she immediately recognised the voice.

'So—this time you've really hit the jackpot.'

The papers slid from her nerveless fingers and her knees shook so much she sank on to the nearest chair. It was that or slide to the ground.

Anxiety and panic slammed through her with the force of an express train. 'What do you want?'

'If you have to ask that then you're a lot stupider than you look.'

'W-we already paid you.' Her confidence fell away and her fingers clenched on the phone. 'A fortune. You promised that would be it—'

'Well, let's just say that circumstances have changed. You're a wealthy lady. This time I want ten million.'

She closed her eyes briefly. 'That's ridiculous.'

'You've snagged the attentions of a billionaire.'

'It isn't my money. I can't—'

'Bad decision.' The voice was harsh. 'Goodbye.'

'Wait!' She stood up, panic and anguish in her tone. 'Don't hang up!'

'Are you going to be reasonable?'

What choice did she have? Her eyes filled and her voice was little more than a whisper. 'Yes. I—I'll do anything—'

There was a cold laugh from the other end of the phone. 'Now you're being sensible. And because I'm in a generous mood I'll give you twenty-four hours to get the money. Then I'll contact you again. And if you tell the police or Santoro, then the deal is off.'

Twenty-four hours?

How was she going to get the money in twenty-four hours? *It wasn't long enough.* She couldn't possibly—

'I won't tell Luc, I promise I won't tell Luc, but—' She broke off as she realised that the connection was dead.

'So what exactly are you not going to tell me?' An icy voice came from the doorway and the phone fell from her fingers with a clatter to join the papers on the floor.

She stared at Luc in horror, wondering just how much he'd heard. 'You're early—'

'Clearly ploughing through obstacles in order to spend more time with my family wasn't a sensible move,' he said flatly, walking into the room and pushing the door shut behind him, hostility and condemnation pulsing from every inch of his powerful frame. 'I have spent the last month jumping through hoops to be the sort of man you want me to be. You accuse me of not being able to communicate and yet time and time again the person with the secrets in this relationship is *you*.'

She could hardly breathe, but her panic was all for Rio. 'I don't have secrets—' She couldn't handle this now. She just needed to be left on her own to think and plan and yet how could she do either when her mind was full of anxiety for her child?

Luc planted himself in front of her, his powerful frame a wall of tension. 'So what is it that you've promised not to tell me and who were you making that promise to?'

For a moment she stared at him, sickened by the icy remoteness she saw in his eyes and the disdainful slant of his beautiful mouth. She wanted to defend herself but how could she when the blackmailer had insisted she didn't tell Luc? What if she told him and something happened to Rio?

She tried to comfort herself with the knowledge that Luc had security staff watching Rio, but she still couldn't relax.

'I can't talk about this now.' She needed to talk to Jason. She needed to go to the school. She needed to pick up her child. Urgently. In a complete fluster, she dropped to her knees to gather up the papers she'd scattered but her hands were shaking so badly she immediately dropped them again. Tears pricked her eyes and she blinked them back. 'Can we go back to Brazil this afternoon?' she blurted out impulsively, tilting her head to look at him. 'All three of us? Please?'

Luc lifted stunned dark eyes from the mess on the floor and stared at her with unconcealed amazement. 'The school term isn't ended yet. You said you wanted to wait until the summer holidays. Those were your terms. Remember?'

'I kn-know what I said,' she stammered, gathering up the sketches she'd dropped and then promptly dropping them again. Her hands were shaking so much she couldn't hold anything. 'I've changed my mind. I want us to go now. As soon as we can.'

If she took Rio out of school, then they could go to the island and he'd be safe there, she reasoned desperately. He'd be surrounded by water and Luc's security team. In a place like that they'd be able to protect him, *keep him safe*.

Luc studied her with a visible lack of comprehension. 'Suddenly you want to fly to Brazil. Why?'

She started picking up papers again, her brain paralysed by terror. 'Why must you always ask so many questions?'

'Perhaps because you're not giving me anything that looks even remotely like an answer,' he ground out, reaching for her and hauling her against him. '*Stop* picking up papers and dropping them again, *stop* avoiding my gaze and stand still for just one minute so that we can *talk*.'

'I can't. Not now.' Not ever. She didn't dare think what might happen to Rio if she told Luc the truth. 'And anyway, there's nothing to say.' Her voice was barely audible and he took such a long time to react that for a moment she wondered whether he'd even heard her.

Then he released her so suddenly that she almost fell. 'Fine.' His tone was ice-cold. 'Clearly I was the one who was crazy to even think we could have a relationship. Go and do whatever it is you have to do that I mustn't find out about. I'm going to the office. I'll be back later to pick Rio up and take him for tea. And then my lawyer will contact you to discuss arrangements for the future. Finally I agree with you. Marriage is not on the agenda. I can't marry a woman whose behaviour I'm not even *close* to understanding.'

She wanted to hurl herself into the safety of his arms.

She wanted to tell him *everything* and let him sort it out the way he'd sorted everything out. But she didn't dare.

So instead she stood there, watching through a haze of tears as he strode out of the room like a man with no intention of ever coming back.

Kimberley wanted to break down and just sob and sob until her heart was empty of emotion and her body was dry, but she knew she couldn't allow herself that luxury. She had to get to her son. *Before anyone else did.*

She made it just as far as the door when the phone rang again.

This time it was the school and they were ringing to say that Rio had gone missing.

Luc strode towards his car, struggling to contain the fierce rage of jealousy that threatened to consume his usually cold and rational approach to life. The guilt on Kimberley's face when she'd dropped the phone had ignited feelings inside him that he had never before experienced. For a wild, primitive moment he'd been tempted to throw her over his shoulder, carry her to his nearest property and lock all the doors so that she could have no contact with the outside world.

No contact with other men.

Because he was completely and utterly sure that it was a man who was causing her to be so secretive.

Hadn't she already told him on several occasions that there was no reason why she shouldn't have another man in her life?

And hadn't he spent the last month trying to prove to her that she didn't *need* another man in her life?

Was that why she'd put that ridiculous ban on sex? Because she was spending her nights with another man?

He uttered a soft curse and wondered why he should be suddenly experiencing a depth of insecurity hitherto completely alien to him.

He'd left Paris earlier than planned, overwhelmed by a sudden inexplicable need to be with Kimberley, only to find her white-faced and clearly horrified to see him. His dreams of an ecstatic romantic reunion had dissolved on the spot. The rare diamond that he'd chosen with such care and hidden securely in his pocket until such time as he deemed it appropriate to present it to his future wife, had remained in his pocket, a cruel reminder of how life with Kimberley never turned out the way he expected.

In fact *nothing* had gone the way he'd planned.

For a man used to nothing short of adulation from the female sex, Kimberley's less than flattering reaction to his arrival had come as a severe shock. But over the past month he'd been convinced on several occasions that she was actually enjoying their time together.

Which simply went to prove that a desperate man was a deluded man, he thought grimly as he strode towards his car.

How had he expected her to react to his early arrival?

So surprised by his unexpected appearance that she'd drop her guard, throw herself into his arms and declare her love?

That she'd show him the same unquestioning devotion she'd offered him at the age of eighteen?

Hardly. As she kept reminding him, she wasn't that person any more. Instead of warmth and affection, she displayed nothing but cool reserve and nothing in her body language suggested that she was missing the physical side of their relationship.

Was that because her affection was given elsewhere?

He ground his teeth at the very thought and wondered what it was that she was hiding from him. Whatever it was had been enough to drain the colour from her cheeks and put a look of raw terror into her green eyes.

As the first punch of jealousy receded and his brain once more clicked into action he frowned, recalling her extreme pallor and the papers scattered over the floor.

He stopped dead, oblivious to the curious glances of his security staff and his chauffeur, who was poised to take him to his next appointment. *The papers had already been on the floor before he'd entered the room.*

With the same single-minded focus and ruthless attention to detail that characterised all his business dealings, Luc applied his mind to every moment of their meeting, searching for clues and answers.

She had been pale from the moment he'd walked into the

room, he reminded himself. He hadn't caused the pallor. The papers had already been on the floor. His unexpected arrival hadn't caused her to drop them.

The only thing she'd dropped when she'd seen him had been the phone.

He frowned as he mentally ran through the exact sequence of events.

Like a woman who was desperate, she'd begged him to take them back to Brazil, even though she'd been the one to insist that Rio needed stability and should finish his term at school before they considered travelling.

Why would she want to go back to Brazil if she had another man in her life?

Something didn't feel right.

Like so many men before him, he cursed fluently and wished that women didn't have to be so extremely complicated and perverse in their behaviour.

At that moment his mobile phone rang and he answered the call immediately, all his senses on full alert when he saw that it was Kimberley's number displayed on the screen.

She whispered three words. 'I need you.'

Where was Luc and when would he come?

Kimberley was huddled on the floor, shaking so badly that she couldn't speak.

Her worst nightmare had come true.

'Calm down and tell me again what the school said—' Jason held a glass of brandy to her lips but she pushed it away, her eyes wild with fear. For a moment she thought she might be swallowed up by panic and then she heard the firm, determined tread of Luc's footsteps on the wooden floor and almost wept again with relief because she needed him badly, even though she knew she wasn't supposed to need him.

He strode into the room, his expression grim as his dark

eyes swept the room. He took in Jason holding the glass and then registered her tear-stained face with a soft curse.

In two strides he was by her side. 'From the beginning,' he commanded in rough tones as he lifted her easily and sat in the nearest chair with her on his lap, 'and this time you're going to leave nothing out.'

For a brief moment Kimberley rested a hand against his chest, feeling the solid strength of hard male muscle under her fingers, allowing herself the luxury of comfort. And then she remembered that she didn't have time for comfort.

'I have to go—' She went to slide off his lap but his arms tightened around her waist, preventing her from moving.

'You're going nowhere.'

'You don't understand—' Almost whimpering with fear, she pushed at his arms, trying to free herself. 'He's been taken.'

Luc stilled. '*Who* has been taken?'

'Rio.' Her eyes were frantic. 'He was supposed to give me twenty-four hours to get the money but the school just phoned and he's disappeared.'

'You are making absolutely no sense.' Luc narrowed his eyes as he tried to decipher her garbled statement. Then he inhaled sharply, his expression suddenly grim. 'The blackmailer has contacted you again? Is that what you're saying?'

Kimberley turned to Jason for support, not knowing what to do or say.

'You want my opinion?' Her friend gave a helpless shrug. 'You need to tell him everything. He might be able to help. We both know that Luc's a nasty bastard when he's crossed.'

'Thanks.' Luc cast an ironic glance at the other man, who gave an apologetic shrug.

'Take it as a compliment. You have assets that we need at the moment.'

'They made me promise not to tell you. What if they find out?' Kimberley was shivering with fear but Luc was totally calm, his handsome face an icy mask as he reached for his phone. Without providing them with any explanation, he made three calls in rapid succession, his tone cold and unemotional as he issued what she assumed to be a string of instructions in his own language. Then he slipped the phone back into his pocket and gave her a gentle shake.

'You should have told me. Do you know nothing about me? Do you think I would allow anyone to take our child?' His tone was rough and his fingers tightened on her arms and she looked at him blankly, too afraid to think straight.

'I suppose not—' Suddenly there was a glimmer of light in the darkness. She'd forgotten how strong Luc was, even though she'd seen the evidence of that strength on several occasions. Even now he was strong. Unlike her, he was showing no sign of panic. Instead he was cold and rational and very much in control.

Jason dumped the glass down on the table. 'How can a child of six go missing from a school?'

Despite the warmth and safety of Luc's arms, Kimberley couldn't stop shivering. 'Because someone took him.'

'Calm yourself, *meu amorzinho*,' Luc urged roughly. 'No one has taken him. It isn't possible. My team have not left his side since I discovered his existence.'

His phone rang suddenly and he answered it immediately, his expression revealing nothing as he listened and responded. He ended the call with a determined stab of one bronzed finger. 'As I thought—all is well. Rio is safe. One of my security team picked him up two minutes ago, just to be on the safe side. You can relax, *minha docura*.'

'They've found him?' Kimberley's voice was a strangled whisper and Luc gave a soft curse and stroked her tangled hair away from her blotched face.

'He had crossed the road to the sweet shop,' he said gruffly, 'apparently to buy me a present to take to the airport. He had much to say to my driver about your plans to surprise me.'

Kimberley blushed. 'We were going to meet you, but you were early—'

His dark eyes were unusually penetrating. 'A mistake I will remember not to make again,' he said softly, pushing her gently off his lap but maintaining a firm grip on her hand as they stood up. 'My team are taking Rio straight back to my hotel. He'll be safe there. I'll take you to him, but first you need to wash your face and practise your smile. We don't want him to know that anything is wrong.'

'But what about the man? He's still out there and he gave me twenty-four hours—'

'It is not your problem,' Luc informed her with the cool confidence of a man totally comfortable in the command position. 'He slipped up when he called you here. We now have his identity and his whereabouts. He'll be dealt with.'

For once she was more than willing to let him take control of the situation.

Something in the grim set of his mouth made her feel almost sorry for the blackmailer but then she reminded herself that the man had threatened her child and deserved to be on the receiving end of Luc's wrath.

She splashed her face in the bathroom and when she came out there were two security staff waiting to escort her to the hotel.

Luc had gone.

CHAPTER ELEVEN

KIMBERLEY spent the rest of the afternoon and evening playing with Rio in the safety of the hotel suite. Despite the comforting presence of Luc's security staff, she didn't let him out of her sight, all too aware that the threat to his safety still remained.

And as the hours passed and there was still no sign of Luc, she suddenly discovered that her anxiety wasn't only confined to the safety of her child.

What if something had happened to Luc?

Finally, long after Rio had been tucked up in bed asleep, Luc walked into the suite and she dropped on to the nearest sofa, worn out with worrying and almost weak with relief.

'Thank goodness—I was *so* worried and no one would tell me where you were.'

'Why were you worried?' His shirt was undone at the collar and he strolled towards her, as cool and unconcerned as ever. 'You have Rio safe with you.'

'I know, but I thought something might have happened to *you*,' she confessed and then almost bit her tongue off as she realised what she'd revealed.

He didn't want her love or affection.

He just wanted their son. And suddenly she knew that she couldn't marry him, no matter how much she wanted to. It wouldn't be fair on Luc. Eventually he would find someone he could love and she didn't want to stand in the way of his happiness.

They'd have to come to some other arrangement.

He stopped in front of her and dragged her gently to her feet.

'I think it's time you learned to trust me, *meu amorzinho*,' he urged, sliding a hand under her chin and forcing her to look at him. 'You accuse me of being controlling, yet there are times when it is good to allow another to take charge and this was one of them. You have proved time and time again that you are capable of running your own life, but I think when it comes to dealing with blackmailers you can safely leave the work to others. You need to learn to delegate.'

His eyes hardened and she caught her breath, hardly daring to ask the question. 'Did you find him?'

His hand dropped to his side and he gave a smile that wasn't altogether pleasant. 'Of course. The problem is solved.'

'Thank you,' she breathed, almost weak with relief. She suddenly discovered that she didn't even want to know what had happened. She was just glad that it was over. 'Thank you so much.'

Luc released her abruptly and raked long fingers through his sleek, dark hair as he paced away from her. 'Before you bestow your gratitude in my direction I should probably tell you that the whole situation was my fault.' His voice was harsh as he turned back to her. 'He made your life a misery because of me, *minha docura*. I am entirely to blame for your recent trauma so you might want to hold on to your thanks.'

She frowned. 'I don't understand—'

'He was an employee of mine. One of my drivers.' Luc's hands dropped to his sides and he walked towards the window, his expression grim and set, his tone flat. 'I fired him.

He was dishonest and I won't tolerate dishonesty in my employees. That was seven years ago.'

Kimberley stared at him. 'I was with you seven years ago.'

'That's right.'

She looked at him blankly, still not understanding. 'But what does that have to do with me?'

He let out a driven sigh. 'He wanted to make money the easy way. You presented him with the opportunity to do that.'

'But *how*? How did he even know about Rio?'

Luc loosened more buttons of his shirt. 'He was my driver. I suspect he overheard something which he then used to his advantage.'

'But I never—' Kimberley broke off and Luc gave a wry smile.

'You never?' he prompted her gently and she lifted a hand to her mouth.

'Oh, God—the very last time I tried to see you, I came to the office and you arranged for a car to take me away. I was terribly upset—I called Jason to ask him if I could stay with him—'

'And naturally you told him why,' Luc finished for her with a dismissive shrug of his broad shoulders. 'I think you have your answer.'

'Then it's *all* my fault,' she whispered in horror and Luc frowned sharply.

'Not true. If it is anyone's fault it is mine, for sending you away that day without even giving you the courtesy of a hearing. And on the other occasions.' He hesitated, his bronzed face unusually pale as he surveyed her stricken expression. 'I am very much to blame for everything that has happened to you and for that I am truly sorry. My only defence is that you were so very different from every other woman I've ever met.'

She gaped at him, so startled and taken aback by the previously unimaginable vision of Luc Santoro *apologising* that she wasn't aware that he'd even taken her hands until he pulled her against him.

'But the thing that makes me most sorry is that I didn't believe you when you said you were being blackmailed. I'm truly sorry that you've had so much worry to cope with alone,' he said roughly, his dark eyes raking her pale face. 'That day you came to my office and asked me for five million dollars; I should have believed you, but I've never been able to think clearly around you. The truth is that I wanted to believe that you were a cold-hearted little gold-digger.'

'But *why?* Why would you want to think a thing like that about someone?' She stared at him in amazement and he spread his hands, as if the answer should be obvious.

'Seven years ago it was the only way I could keep myself from following you and bringing you back. But I should have known better. You were never interested in possessions. It wasn't until recently that I realised that you truly had no idea just how wealthy I am—'

She bit her lip, more than a little embarrassed that she'd been so naïve. 'To be honest, I'd never really given it any thought.'

She'd never been interested in Luc the businessman. *Only Luc the man.*

'Unlike every other woman I've ever been with, all of whom thought about little else,' he informed her, a hard edge to his voice. 'In contrast, the only thing you've ever asked me for is conversation. You're not interested in material things, so I should have known that when you told me about Rio you were telling the truth. I should have listened to you but unfortunately my temper is as hot as my libido.'

She blushed. 'I can understand that you were still angry with me,' she conceded hastily, more than willing to forgive him. 'I did spend a great deal of your money. Which was probably wrong of me, but I was very upset and scared about the future and I badly wanted to be able to stay at home and look after our baby.'

'You spent next to nothing compared to your predecessors,' he informed her in a dry tone and she blinked in astonishment.

'I bought a *flat*.'

'Which has turned out to be an excellent investment,' he pointed out with some amusement. 'I have had girlfriends who have spent a similar amount expanding the contents of their wardrobes. It appears that the flat has more than trebled in value since you first bought it.'

It was typical of Luc to have already discovered that fact, she thought dryly. 'But if you truly thought I was a gold-digger, why did you want me back in your bed? I never understood that. You'd so obviously had enough of me when we parted seven years ago.'

He grimaced. 'I wish that was the case, but sadly the complete opposite was true.'

She stilled. 'But you drove me away.'

'That's right.'

'You'd *definitely* had enough of me—'

'I doubt I would ever have enough of you, *meu amorzinho*. And that was the very reason I had to make you leave.'

She felt thoroughly confused. All these years she'd made certain assumptions and it seemed now that she'd been wrong. 'You knew I'd leave?'

'Of course—' His smile was self-mocking. 'You were very possessive. I knew that if I was photographed with another woman that would be the end for you. And us.'

'I can't believe you did that.' She struggled to find her voice. 'I was *so* hurt.'

He flinched as though she'd hit him. 'I know and for that I am truly sorry. If it makes it any better, it was all staged. I let the photographer do his stuff and then spent the rest of the evening getting blind drunk. I never touched another woman when we were together.'

She lifted a hand and rubbed the frown between her eyes. 'You hated the fact I was so affectionate, hated the fact that I loved you—because you didn't feel the same way about me.'

He gave a short laugh that was totally lacking in humour. 'You're wrong. I felt *exactly* the same way about you and those feelings scared me.'

Luc, *scared*?

There was a long painful silence while she stared at him. 'You felt the same way I did?'

'That's right.'

Her heart thudded against her chest. 'I *loved* you.'

He tensed slightly. 'I know.'

She licked her lips. 'You accused me of acting—'

'Some men will say anything rather than accept that he's been well and truly hooked by a woman.' Luc ran a hand over the back of his neck, visibly discomfited by the admission. 'I guess I'm one of those men. I didn't know how to handle the situation. For the first time in my life I found myself seriously out of my depth.'

She stared at him. 'You're saying you felt the same way about me?'

'Why do you think I refused to see you on those three occasions? I've always considered myself to be a self-disciplined man but that went out of the window when I met you. I didn't trust myself to turn you away. I was relieved when you spent all that money because it meant that I was finally able to bracket you with all the other women I'd ever been with. It made it easier to push you away.'

'I don't understand.' Her voice was little more than a whisper as she tried to comprehend what he was telling her. 'If you loved me, why did you want to push me away?'

He inhaled sharply. 'Because I didn't want to be in love. I've spent my life avoiding emotional entanglements and I succeeded very well until you came along. I was always careful to pick the same type of woman. Cold, hard and with an eye set firmly on my money. I suppose, in a way, it was a guarantee. I knew there was no chance that I'd ever fall in love with a woman like that so I was perfectly safe. But I made a mistake with you. A big mistake.'

'What's wrong with being in love if it's mutual?' She stared at him in confusion. 'I *adored* you.'

There was a long silence and she saw a shadow cross his hard, handsome face.

He paced over to the window, keeping his back to her as if speaking was suddenly extraordinarily difficult. 'My father loved my mother so much and when she died his entire life fell apart. I watched it happen. I saw a strong man shrivel to nothing and become weak. He no longer wanted to live and he lost interest in everything, including me.' Luc's voice was flat. 'I was thirteen years old and it certainly wasn't a good advertisement for the benefits of love. My father ceased to function. His business folded. We lost our home. And finally he died.'

Kimberley stilled, appalled and saddened. And her heart ached for how he must have suffered as a boy, losing both his parents at such a young, impressionable age. She looked at the stiff set of his broad shoulders and wanted to go to him. *Wanted to hug him tight.* But she sensed that he didn't want her comfort. 'How did he die?'

Luc didn't turn, his eyes still fixed on a point outside the window. 'To be honest, I think he just didn't care enough to live. He gave up.'

She stared at his back helplessly, for the first time feeling as though she'd been given some insight into what made him the person he was. 'And you vowed that was never going to happen to you—'

'And it never did.' He turned, his dark eyes fixed on hers with shimmering intensity. 'Never even came close until I met you. And what I felt for you frightened me so much I refused to acknowledge it, even to myself.'

She swallowed. 'I wish I'd known about your childhood. I wish you'd *talked* to me—'

'I didn't want to talk. I just wanted to run a mile. I'd vowed that it was never going to happen to me. *That I would never make myself that vulnerable.* My father went from being a man with energy and drive to little more than a shell. We lost everything virtually overnight. Maria gave me a home. She was like a mother to me.'

And she guessed that he'd repaid that debt many times over.

'I still think you should have told me.'

He gave a wry smile. 'I didn't tell anyone anything, *meu amorzinho*. That's how I kept myself safe.'

She curled her fingers into her palms. 'So when I turned up at your office six weeks ago—'

'I couldn't resist the temptation to see you one more time and, having seen you, I couldn't resist the temptation to get you into my bed one more time,' he confessed with brutal frankness. 'I convinced myself that two weeks would be enough to cure me. Then I convinced myself that just a little longer would do the trick. I'm not good at being without you, *meu amorzinho*.'

She gazed at him, unable to suppress the bubble of happiness inside her. 'I never even guessed you felt that way.'

'I followed you to England,' he pointed out dryly, 'which should have told you something.'

'I thought it was just sex—'

'*Not* just sex,' he assured her, 'and the last month should have proved that. But if you still don't believe me you can talk to my board of directors, who are currently wondering if I'm ever going to work again. I have been absent from the office for so long they're all becoming extremely jittery.'

She chewed her lip, hardly daring to ask the question that needed to be asked. 'And what about now—' her voice cracked '—are you cured, Luc?'

Luc fixed her with his dark, possessive gaze. 'You really have to ask me that?' His accent was strangely thick, as if he couldn't quite get his tongue around the words that needed to be said. 'In the past month I have thought only of you and what you need in a relationship. I have talked until my throat is sore and told you *everything* about myself. I have expressed thoughts that I didn't even know I was thinking. But, most of all, I have ignored the fact that you only have to walk into a room and I want to strip you naked. You have stayed fully clothed for an entire month and I haven't so much as kissed you on the lips. I have done for you what I've never done for any woman before. And yet *still* you ask me if I love you?'

Suddenly Kimberley just wanted to smile and smile. 'I thought you just wanted to marry me because of Rio—'

'I want to marry you because I love you and because I can't live without you,' he confessed with a groan, pulling her against him. 'And if I was a decent sort of guy I'd be saying that I love you too much to marry you unless you love me. But, as you've pointed out so many times in the past, I'm ruthless and entirely self-seeking and don't understand the word no, so I'm going to keep on at you until you say yes.'

He sounded so much like his usual self that she laughed. 'Controlling again, Luc?' Her eyes twinkled suggestively. 'The handcuffs are still in my bag. Perhaps I should use them again. It isn't good for you to have everything your own way.'

'If it's any consolation, I am suffering badly for the way I treated you,' he confessed in a raw tone. 'It tortures me to think of how alone and afraid you were and that I was the cause of it. I don't know how you managed—'

'Well, your credit cards certainly helped,' she muttered and he gave an agonized groan.

'And you even kept the receipts for everything you bought. Do you know how that made me feel? To know that you felt the need to itemise everything?'

'I'm used to watching what I spend,' she said simply and then gave a rueful smile. 'And, I suppose, deep down I felt guilty spending your money. But you'd called all the shots and it was a way of taking some of the control back.'

His own eyes gleamed dark in response. 'Once we're safely married you can take control any time you like,' he assured her huskily, sliding his hands into her hair and tilting her face to his. 'But, in the meantime, I need you to put me out of my misery. I never dreamt that asking a woman to marry me could be so traumatic. No wonder I've avoided commitment for so long.'

'I didn't know you were asking—I thought you were telling.'

'I'm *trying* to ask; it's just that asking is all very new to me,' he confessed in a smooth tone that suggested that he had absolutely no intention of changing his ways in the near future.

'Like compromise and conversation,' she teased and he gave a tortured groan.

'*Don't* tease me—just give me an answer.' His dark head lowered and his mouth brushed against hers. 'Are you going to say yes or do you have still more challenges and tests for me to pass before you'll agree to tie yourself to me for ever?'

For ever.

How could two words sound so good?

'I think you've more than passed the test,' she whispered as she slid her arms round his neck. 'And the answer is yes.'

'And do you think, if I really concentrate on compromise and conversation, that you might manage to love me back one day, the way you used to love me?'

'I already do,' she said softly, standing on tiptoe and kissing him again. 'You were absolutely right when you said that no other man had ever matched up to what we shared. I've never found anyone who made me feel the way you do.'

'Seriously?' He looked stunned, as if he couldn't quite allow himself to believe what she was saying. 'You still love me?'

'I've never stopped loving you. Although I'm worried about what such a confession will do to your already massively over-inflated ego.'

He gave a delighted laugh and pulled her hard against him. 'So if I put a ring on your finger straight away, can we drop the "no sex" routine because, frankly, abstinence is something else that I don't excel at.'

'Me neither,' she confessed breathlessly, her cheeks heating at the hard, male feel of him against her, 'and there's no need to wait for a ring.'

'You're going to wear the ring,' he told her in his usual tone of authority, reaching into his jacket pocket and removing a velvet box. 'The ring says "hands off, she's mine" to any other man who happens to glance in your direction. I want you well and truly labelled so that there can be no mistake.'

'Not possessive at all then, Luc,' she teased and then gasped as he flipped open the box and the stunning diamond winked and sparkled at her. 'Oh, it's *beautiful* '

'It's worth a small fortune, not that you care about things like that,' he added hastily. 'I bought it in Paris when I decided that I absolutely wasn't going to take no for an answer.' He slid it on to her finger and then pulled her back into his arms.

'And if I *had* said no?'

He stroked her hair away from her face. 'I don't understand no,' he reminded her in husky tones as he bent his head to claim her mouth again. 'I had a *very* limited education.'

She felt her head swim and her legs turn to liquid and forced herself to pull away briefly before she completely lost the ability to communicate. 'In that case I'd better say yes—' the look in his eyes made her breathless '—but you have to promise not to be too controlling or I might be forced to handcuff you to the bed again so that I can have my own way.'

His eyes gleamed. 'In that case, *meu amorzinho*,' he murmured huskily, 'it's only fair to warn you that I'm planning on being controlling any moment now.'

Her heart missed a beat and she ran her tongue over her lower lip. 'So perhaps we ought to move this conversation through to the bedroom.'

Luc gave a low, sexy laugh and scooped her into his arms. 'I'm finding the whole concept of conversation increasingly more appealing with practice.'

And he walked through to the bedroom and kicked the door closed behind them.

HARLEQUIN *Presents*

Legally wed, but he's never said... "I love you."

They're

Wedlocked!

Where
marriages are
made in haste...
and love
comes later....

This December,

Emily Vaillon was driven to leave her husband a year
ago. She couldn't stay with a man who didn't love
her—especially when she was pregnant. Now Luc
is back, demanding to see his son....

THE FRENCHMAN'S
CAPTIVE BRIDE

by Chantelle Shaw

#2594 On sale December.

Look out for more *Wedlocked!* marriage stories
coming in Harlequin Presents:

THE FORCED BRIDE by Sara Craven
#2597 Coming in January!

www.eHarlequin.com